Inside
Ant's Belly

A collection of stories for young people

edited by

Merle Collins and Marva Buchanan

ISBN 0 901291 36 6

First published 1994
Printed in the United Kingdom by York Publishing Services

Contents

Acknowledgements

'The Visit' was previously published in Merle Collins, *Rain Darling*, The Women's Press, 1990.

'Karima' was published in *Border Lines*, Serpent's Tail, 1993.

'The Canebreakers' was previously published in Jacob Ross, *Song for Simone*, Karia Press, 1986.

'The Dead Men Who Lost Their Bones' was previously published in *Drum*, South Africa, October 1980.

About the editors

Merle Collins is Grenadian. She lives in London and is a Senior Lecturer in Caribbean Studies at the University of North London. Her published work includes two poetry collections, *Because the Dawn Breaks* (The Women's Press, 1985) and *Rotten Pomerack* (Virago, 1992), a novel, *Angel* (The Women's Press, 1987), and a collection of short stories, *Rain Darling* (The Women's Press, 1990). She is also co-editor of the collection *Watchers and Seekers: Creative Writing by Black Women in Britain* (The Women's Press, 1987).

Marva Buchanan was born in Jamaica and grew up in Britain. She lives in London and is a teacher of English and Drama, currently working for the African-Caribbean Attainment Project in the London Borough of Waltham Forest.

Illustrator's note

The cover illustration represents a disjointed 'room' with walls and ceiling depicting maps of the areas featured in the stories. This is to portray the state of exile; of 'separateness' from a culture. The head incorporates the faces of a West Indian man with an Asian woman. The person is writing while looking out of the green window on the left, which represents Britain. The red hibiscus is symbolic of a tropical culture left behind. The 'shadow' of the person on the right carries images, perhaps memories, or dreams, of places across the sea. The paper being written on is flying from the table – possibly a letter or a piece of writing about a different place. The footprints across the top of the illustrations indicate the movement of immigration.

Introduction

In Grenada there is a saying, 'What is joke for schoolchildren is death for crapaud'. This assumes that schoolchildren will sometimes crowd around a frog (crapaud) which they see in a drain, laughing and pointing. While the frog tries to escape, the children pounce, pelt, and may even stone it to death. Crapaud has a different way of living, which they do not respect. This is not always the case. We know one schoolboy who sits for so long in the garden looking at the way insects and animals function that he reminds us of another saying, 'If you have patience, you will see inside ant's belly!' Can you imagine? That's a lot of patience.

The stories in this collection encourage you not to stone the crapaud, but to try to see inside ant's belly, to think of different ways of experiencing the world.

Some of them are stories of things you have perhaps experienced. Some may not be your experience, but might well be what people you meet every day have experienced. They are the kinds of stories that you can write if you listen to yourself, listen to others, and look at what is going on around you.

Even as you read, there is a Chantelle being 'accommodated' somewhere. Perhaps her story sounds like yours. Many of the stories focus on migration and its impact. The writers speak of movement from country to town and from city to city. Because they are living here in Britain, they speak of the physical and emotional journeys involved in moving from India to Pakistan, from Jamaica to England, from home to university. Perhaps you have your own story of movement. Perhaps you, too, have felt like part of an 'invisible mass in the back row'.

We want you to recognise yourselves and others, but we also want you to enjoy the writing. There are many things you are sure to encounter when reading the stories in this anthology. You will encounter themes of exile, loss and separation.

In 'The Shadow and the Substance', there is the sense of estrangement from family and from a sibling of a similar age group. This emotional estrangement can also be found in some of the other stories. In 'Accommodated', Chantelle finds it difficult to communicate with her mother. In 'Yemar', Lemn Sisay creates an environment which we instinctively know will ultimately prove uncomfortable for the prospective adopted child. In Aamer Hosein's story, the protagonist Karima also feels a sense of discomfiture in a family environment which becomes hostile and unsupportive. In 'Karima', there is also an exploration of that sense of estrangement – exile – with which we are more familiar. This is the separation from country, from a familiar geographical space. The style of the writing explores both the writer's own sense of alienation: 'yet again my stories hadn't earned me the fare home' and the exile of the protagonist, Karima: ' . . . I suddenly felt strange, and foreign, and poor'. This sense of being torn from a familiar environment is also present in the stories 'Diary of Home' and Claudette Williams' 'Invisible Mass of the Back Row'.

The origins of the characters in the stories are as varied and as mixed as those of the writers. They – the writers – speak with authoritative voices because they have experienced or borne close witness to the situations described. The stories refer to real-life occurrences such as the 1947 secession of Bangladesh from Pakistan, the 1960s arrival in Britain of Caribbean children to join parents who had migrated earlier and the destruction of African lives under South Africa's system of apartheid. You will notice also that an often painful outcome of separation is the loss of parents or of children.

In Mandla Langa's 'Dead Men Who Lost Their Bones', twin sisters Clementine and Benedicta lose their father and mother. What they hear 'in the snarling silence of the midnight hour' are 'Words like, *Mama, Papa, Our House.*' In 'Yemar', the mother, who is forced to give up her child for adoption, feels this loss acutely. Chantelle, in 'Accommodated', has her family home replaced by the children's home run by the Social

Services. The mechanisms of the Social Services feature in all three stories. In 'Dead Men Who Lost Their Bones', the children end up in a home run by a religious Order.

In the stories, even in the face of very difficult and painful situations, the characters show tremendous resilience and determination to overcome their adversities. Throughout these stories, they display a willingness to persist, spurred on by a memory, sometimes vague, of having at some time been loved. Kamala, in 'Red Hibiscus', finally shakes off her alcohol dependency after receiving from home a postcard with a picture of the hibiscus flower, a positive symbol of hope. The twins in Mandla Langa's story leave us feeling that one day they will be sufficiently in control of their own existence to discover the truth about their father's death. Joan Riley's Chantelle never ceases to hope for a reunion with her mother and actively plans towards that end. In spite of the difficulties experienced, her optimistic love for her mother remains.

The sense of enduring love is expressed in all of the stories. There is the love of a mother for her son, children for their parents, and, in Jacob Ross's 'The Canebreakers', a woman for her young brother and two young people for each other.

The writers examine feelings of both joy and pain within these stories, though undoubtedly the subject matter is often solemn. The humour is subtle and at times ironic. In 'The Visit', both Catherine and her mother declare their intention never to repeat the experiment of even temporary displacement. Catherine, in England, states, 'Never me again'. These same lines are echoed by Miriam, her mother, once she is safely back in Grenada.

We hope you will feel the joy of working with words to write your own stories, whether the theme is pain or joy. All the contributors enjoy working with words, and that is an essential part of what their stories convey. Part of their joy comes from the ability to tell stories in a wide range of linguistic mixes and techniques, reflecting their varied cultural backgrounds.

We thought of providing you with a glossary explaining words which might be unfamiliar to you. However, we feel it would be a much better venture for you to do some personal research into the languages and cultures represented here. For instance, could you tell which were the Zulu sentences and which the Afrikaans in Mandla Langa's story? Do you know who is Suchitra Mitra, mentioned in 'Red Hibiscus'?

These writers have all followed a trail of varied experiences. They have waited and have now seen inside ant's belly. Now with their words they offer you a glimpse.

Enjoy. Write your own stories. Perhaps one day you will tell the world what you saw 'inside ant's belly'.

Merle Collins and Marva Buchanan

The Shadow
and the Substance

Simmone Miller

The Shadow and the Substance

'Why the hell are you going behind God's back? Why are you going so far away? Eh? You know there are plenty plenty options locally or in London. Studying in these far far places is madness.'

I was anxious, excited and frightened as I went to sleep that night. I would be somewhere new and someone new as from the morning. Given the choice, I wouldn't turn back again. I could only hope that I'd never have to turn back with regret, as I often did in my life; always wishing for something different, something better, something more. It seemed to me that I was always the one who was confused, indecisive, unfocused, unsure. My mind would be made up, but as soon as I compared myself to the likes of 'her' and considered 'her' opinion – whatever the situation, my thoughts would become clouded once more. It was almost as if I didn't have a mind of my own and, looking back, it makes me feel sad.

I lay on my back and stared into the blackness. I could only see dark blotches, nothing distinguished. The morning arrived sooner than I had anticipated, then everything became clear. I smiled a little as I glanced towards her bed. I had shared a room, private space, with my sister for as long as I could remember. Nothing in our room really belonged to me. The occasional soft snore reminded me that I would soon have my own space.

I don't think my feelings towards my sister were those of hatred; it was more of a yearning to be accepted as an individual. People tended to treat us like twins; it was always 'You two', 'Those two', 'You both' or 'The second one'. She was 'The first one'. She was the figure, always moving. I became her shadow, always following. I always found myself desperately trying to be her, but I also knew this had to stop. It would stop as from today.

'I've written you a list of all the things you should have packed. I bet there's something you've forgotten, knowing you.

I bought you a small gift for you to take with you; I hope you like it.'

I knew she loved me, but I was also aware that I was even more like her than the face which looked back at her from the mirror. The funny thing was, she respected me and would do anything to help. She was thoughtful, kind, a difficult person to hate. So I hated her – sometimes.

She had given me a little electric alarm clock, as she had always woken me up in the mornings. I felt bad. I resented her so much. It hurt so bad. It really hurt.

The worst part was saying goodbye to my family, a brief and tearful goodbye. The taxi would be here soon and I would be able to put all this behind me. I couldn't ignore the fact that I would be leaving with a lot of bitterness inside, which had been there for a large part of my life.

The taxi-driver seemed to take a long time to load my luggage into the car boot. I was so relieved when I heard the boot door slam shut. I sat impatiently whilst my family stood motionless on the doorstep. I could see that everyone was desperately trying to hide any sign of emotional weakness; everyone, including me. I could feel my sister trying to catch my attention but I forced myself to keep my head down. Only as the taxi moved off did I turn back and wave.

Facing the front, I could see the driver's eyes fixed on me in the mirror. The corners of his eyes creased. I guess he smiled. I looked quickly away. He was probably used to seeing situations like this. There was silence. I had nothing to say; it was all written on my face. I was sure it was all obvious. I felt naked. I felt cold. This man was probably asking himself why I was so desperate to get away from what looked like a loving family – she's ungrateful and selfish. Maybe I am. I must be.

I came to the conclusion that my sister cannot help being who she is. It is not her problem if I find so much fault with her. I cannot accuse her of not trying to encourage or help me simply because that would be untrue. So if things just naturally turned out better for her, then I should be happy for her, and most importantly, learn from that. Having said that, it is not so easy in reality. I often wonder what goes through her mind; particularly when I reach a peak of disappointment. I ask myself if she is laughing at me. I have always imagined her laughing at me in the dark, alone, knowing that no one can hear or see her. Sometimes I am certain of this.

The taxi-driver, whilst unloading the boot, mumbled the fare, which I scrambled to find. I was left standing at the coach station, feeling tired already and I could feel self pity welling up. I told myself: 'For God's sake pull yourself together', and with that I decided to move towards the ticket office. I deliberately made my mind blank of all that had happened that morning, I would feel stupid if I broke down in tears whilst purchasing my ticket.

Standing at Bay D, I began to observe the people around me. I didn't notice anyone who looked like a student. Just what looked to be middle-aged, middle-class people waiting for a coach. No one did anything to invite particular attention. It was fairly quiet. Perhaps because it was Sunday.

'Make sure you get on the right coach. Don't be hasty; just take your time. Someone is bound to help you with your luggage. As soon as you get there, ring. Don't forget to ring us, you hear me!'

The voices from home returned. I shook them off. Throughout the journey I felt numb, overwhelmingly numb. I didn't think, cry, sigh, nothing. I just sat and stared out of the window, not absorbing the view or taking in someone else's conversation. I willed my thoughts to be on hold until the coach pulled up at Bristol coach station and I had to collect my luggage.

This was really it. I was in Bristol. I had made it in more ways than one: I had been accepted by the university and I had also broken free from the boundaries back home. So why didn't I feel happy? This question repeated itself several times inside my head, until I realised I had been standing in the same position for some time. What was holding me back? This day was going to come eventually – I thought I was prepared, but obviously I wasn't. There was no familiar voice reassuring me, fussing over me, lecturing me. There was no one. I would now have to do all those things for myself. I would have to adjust to that.

Having lived away from home for some time now has enabled me to stand back and look at myself more clearly. I have become my own person, no longer just a silhouette. The distance between me and my sister has allowed me to step out of that fantasy. I can walk alone. I have found that self-reliance is reliable and consistent. It doesn't choose a time that suits it best. It is always there. It took me over eighteen years to realise that. I learnt that the hard way.

'There's a phone call for you; it's your sister.'

Several months ago, if I had tried to predict my response to this phone call, I would have said that there would be reluctance, on my part, to go to the phone.

I race down three flights of stairs as quickly as I can. Only afterwards do I wonder if I have locked myself out of my room. Picking up the receiver, I gasp for my breath back. My sister picks up on my excitement and an energetic conversation begins.

———

Simmone Miller was born in London of Caribbean parents. She is a Humanities student at the University of West England. She has been writing poetry for approximately six years and some of her poems were published in her High School magazine.

Accommodated

Joan Riley

Accommodated

It was Shaz's fault why I ended up in this grotty room, 'accommodated' is what my social worker call it, but I could think of a few other things I'd call it instead. I'm Chantelle Jameson by the way and Shaz, that's Sharon Gilbert, was my best friend. Guess if I was honest I'd say she was the only friend I ever had. She isn't like the other girls at Manor Park School, all posh with their trendy gear and expensive trainers. She's dead pretty though and she looks about eighteen when she puts on her make-up and the strapless dress her boyfriend Nige bought her for her birthday last year. Even some of the snooty girls that live in the big houses on the avenue wants to be friends with her, but Shaz chose me for her best friend.

I haven't seen her for a while though, haven't seen anybody 'cept my social worker and that bloke down at child guidance; not since Mum refused to have me back home and they put me in this hostel place. That's cos I'm too shame to go to school in case the other girls find out about me being chucked out of home.

I suppose I like Shaz cos she's a bit like me really, poor. I don't look anything like her mind, I'm sort of fat and I've had this problem with zits for ages now. We both come from crummy Sebastian Park Estate, take free school meals and never get to go abroad on school journeys. Her dad's been out of work since the cable works closed down two years ago. Her mum works part time though, got a cleaning job down at the bookies, so she don't have to wear clothes from the Hospice shop like me. Shaz says her mum's on the fiddle cos the Income Support people don't know about her job, but her mum says is the only way she can manage.

Shaz tells me all her secrets, says she can trust me not to blab. I mean who would I tell? None of the other girls talk to me and Mum's too busy to care what I have to say.

I guess that's how this whole thing started, when she told me about going all the way with Nige. Her mum was real upset about that see. Shaz says she was shouting at her and her dad even belted her one. That's how come they got the social worker down. When they had that row she just went straight round to Nige's and spent the night there and next thing she gets home and there's this police woman and social worker and they were telling her about how it was illegal because Nige was twenty-one and she was only fifteen and that he could go to prison for raping her and all that.

That's when she had to go down by the Social Service Office. This woman who came to see her, told her dad, Shaz was at risk and that she had to come down there and be helped. Shaz couldn't make no sense of that and her dad threatened to belt her again if she didn't do what the woman said. Shaz reckoned he was scared cos the woman could set the law on him and he'd been doing some stuff at the building site down by the docks without signing off. At any rate she had to go down the office once a week after school and see some other woman; till she got dead cheesed and lied and said she never had sex with Nige in the first place and she wasn't going to see him any more.

Personally I think she was afraid her dad was going to kick her out, like he did with her big sister two years ago; cos when the social worker said he wasn't suppose to hit her anymore, her dad said they had to take her in care and make sure she behave. That's how Shaz found out that they didn't do that no more. The social worker told her dad, there was this new law and that they could only accommodate her . . . you know, find her somewhere to live and give her pocket money and that . . . just so she'd be safe.

That bit really caught my interest, the fact you could get out of home just like that. I have this problem with my mum's boyfriend see. It's not the sort of thing I could tell a single soul. I felt a bit mean about not telling Shaz specially as we'd sworn to tell each other everything when we first got to be friends. It's a good thing she talk too much to notice I never have anything to say.

You know, Mum and me, we were real happy together when her last boyfriend left – Derrick his name was, and he couldn't stand the sight of me. He used to work for the council, digging graves or something gross like that. He was always tracking dirt all over the carpet and insisting that I get the bucket and scrubbing brush and clean it, and Mum would just stand there and let him boss me around. She's always like that when she has a boyfriend. Just stand around looking vacant and let them do whatever they want. Mind you, Derrick was better than some of the others, at least he used to give me a fiver to make myself scarce on Saturday night when he wanted to have sex with Mum.

I think Derrick lasted about a year before he got fed up with Mum and started having other girlfriends as well. Then Mum got fed up with him and started to argue because he hardly gave her any money, and one day he just up and left in the middle of a ding dong row.

I was nearly thirteen then and we were alone for about six months before Mum got Dismal Dennis who she's with now. She used to do all sorts with me, like going to McDonald's on Saturday after the shopping and we even went to Southend-on-Sea once. I remember how she used to try and help me with my homework, though she wasn't too good with that cos she used to bunk off school when she was little. And she even dressed in her good blue dress – the one she wears to Bingo – and came to parents' evening at school. It's funny how Mum always seem to have more money and time when she don't have a boyfriend. Mind you I can't see her going without one for long, and it's no use me trying to say anything to her in case she lose her temper and belt me one for going on at her. The trouble is Mum's got nothing else to do and she get bored. There ain't no jobs round here see and I guess it can't be fun for her stuck in our flat on the twelfth floor at Conway Towers – the worst block on the whole estate – day in day out. We got rehoused there seven years ago, cos me dad, who was with us then, kept falling behind with the rent on our other flat. Mum don't really have no friends, though she sometimes talk to the woman who got rehoused two flats along from us with her three kids. She don't like the people who live in our block cos she says they're a rough lot. The council only put trouble-makers and people who fall behind with their rent in the Tower.

Dismal D – Shaz nicknamed him that cos she said he was so fat it was dismal, well, he wasn't too bad when he first started going out with Mum. He used to always bring me something . . . you know like chocolate or flowers, he even brought me make-up once. Shaz and I had a right giggle over that. I mean who wears shocking-pink lipstick these days?

I guess the trouble really started when Mum fell pregnant. Mind you I never really liked DD right from the first. It was because of him Shaz stopped coming round by ours. She said he gave her the creep and he was a real groper. Not that he did any of that to me then, and anyway Shaz can be a bit of a tease when she gets a mind to.

Mum had a bad time when she was pregnant with our Ian, she just got sort of droopy and she was always being sick. Then she wouldn't let DD sleep with her any more and he had to stay on the couch. He kept telling Mum he didn't mind and that he just wanted her and the baby to be safe. YUK!

Mum would get all sort of weepy and say how nice it was to find a man who had respect for women. Me, I was just sick of all of it. I used to talk to Shaz about running away, but then it got so that I was too busy and anyway I was too scared to do anything like that, after that programme they had on the telly bout them kids that ended up on the game and got beat up and all sorts.

I had to do all the cooking and the cleaning and everything with Mum sick all the time. That's when DD decided it was all too much for me. I was glad at first. I mean what with my paper-round and doing everything in the house I never seemed to have no time to hang out with Shaz, and I was getting a bit worried in case she found someone else to go round with.

DD wasn't a half bad cook, and I was thankful for that, because between Mum and me we could barely boil an egg. He got this old cookery book from a mate of his and used to do all sort of fancy stuff out of it. The only trouble was afterwards when I had to do the washing up. Our kitchen's real small and when two people is in there you can't cross from one side to the other without touching. Well DD would wait until I was doing the washing up, then he would sort of sidle up behind me, and wedge himself between the fridge and the wall with me trapped up against the sink. Then he would sort of bump up against me. He would reach across me to take things from the drainer and kind of keep touching my breast accidentally on purpose like.

To start with, when I told him to give over he would stop, but then as Mum got bigger and more stroppy about him touching *her*, he would start to argue and say he was only being friendly. I suppose I should have said something to Mum, but she just didn't seem to want to hear when I said anything bad about DD. I think she thought I was jealous she was having his baby.

Anyway I thought things would get better once the baby came, but then Mum went and got depressed and kept having to go down the hospital. When they got fed up of her . . . said something about her not being motivated . . . they just gave her a bunch of pills that made her dopey all the time and send her home. All she ever seem to do was feed the baby and sleep.

Shaz was spending a lot of time with Nige so I couldn't hang out with her so often, and the other kids on the estate didn't want to know. I suppose it's because the girls were all into boyfriends and no boy was about to look at me . . . at least no decent looking one. Not that I minded. Dismal Dennis was bad enough without getting some boy with B.O., slobbering all over me. I suppose that why I just hung around home.

I guess that's when DD really started to get on bad. You know start touching me up and saying things. Sometimes I'd lose my rag and tell him where to get off, but he'd get spiteful and pinch me or give me a wallop. Sometimes he went so far as to tell Mum I'd given him cheek and she'd start on me as well.

You know it got so that I couldn't wait to get to school just to get out of that mad house. Not that me being punctual improved my work any. I mean school was still boring, and I still didn't understand the first thing about science; but now I couldn't even concentrate on English and that's my best subject. All I could think about was how, come evening, I'd have to go back to that flat and DD would start pawing me as soon as Mum turned her back.

Mrs Rushmore my history teacher, she's ever so smashing, was beginning to get a bit worried about me, cos she said I wasn't paying attention and I looked like I had something that was worrying me. I gave her some story about Mum not being well since the baby, but I nearly died at the thought she might find out about DD. Life was bad enough without *that* getting round school.

I'm sort of shy normally, not like Shaz who've got bags of confidence, but I suppose I must have gotten worse cos even Shaz started complaining that I was getting boring. Mind you it might have been cos I told her Nige was a user. I mean, is not *my* fault he's gone and got some girl on the estate pregnant and Shaz's mum freaked when she found out she was still seeing him. Anyway I couldn't tell her about DD cos she'd have thought I was a real wimp for not standing up to him. Shaz was never afraid of anything . . . except her dad in a temper.

Things might have been alright home, if DD hadn't gotten laid off from his job with the gas board. He was a fitter you see and he used to earn good money. Not that Mum ever saw much of it. She was still claiming benefit cos he never gave her no money to speak of.

Mum had started going to some woman's group down at the community hall Wednesday and Friday afternoons, when the lifts were working in our block. She'd wrap up Ian in one of those cellular blanket things and cart him with her cos they had someone to look after the little kids. It was the health visitor who put her up to it. Said getting out of the flat would cheer her up no end. Not that I ever noticed the difference.

The trouble is that Mum got so that she needed to go to the group, and now he was laid off, DD wanted her around home all the time. When he started rowing Mum would just take her pills and ignore him; then he'd start to get all spiteful with me. This last holiday was the worst time, with Shaz round at Nige's house and me being stuck in the flat with nothing to do. Mind you I still never expected what happened last Friday. Just when I was thinking I could just about keep DD under control as well. I'd worked it out see and I'd started telling DD how I was going to set the law on him and he started getting a bit less obvious. But since he's been laid off, he'd been a real pain around home. He even started knocking Mum about, and just before we broke up for Easter he gave me a bit of a black eye.

I used some of Mum's make up to try and hide it, but Miss Fallows – she's our head of year and dead grumpy – made me wash it off. Mrs Rushmore, bless her heart, wanted to know if I'd had an accident, so I told her I wasn't paying attention and walked into a lamp-post. Shaz didn't believe a word of it though. She guessed right off that DD had done it and she told me I was a fool to let him get away with it. Shaz was all for calling that child-line number on the parent notice-board in the school hall; but I didn't really have the guts. I was getting kind of scared of DD but I didn't want no social worker snooping around, cos then Mum would get in trouble for not telling the benefit office that she and DD was living together. And besides I kept thinking bout what happened to Sharon King in the fifth year, when it came out about her and her step-father. Everybody knew about it and she didn't half get teased. Her mum had to find her another school, cos she refused to come after a bit.

Anyway, as I was saying, I thought I had DD under control after that, but then he had that big row with Mum that last Friday. Just cos she wanted him to give me some money for the launderette. DD was stomping around muttering about how

Mum was ungrateful and I didn't have no respect. I was glad it was the last day of the holiday cos I didn't think I could take another day of Dismal Dennis in a temper. Weekends are alright see. He's down by the bookies all day Saturday and I go round by Shaz's in the evening; and Sunday he's down the pub with his mates of the day.

I was just thinking about going down by the library for the afternoon, when DD went stomping out the front door. I was so relieved I washed out Ian's dirty clothes and changed the water in his bucket without Mum having to ask.

There was a film I wanted to see on the telly in the afternoon, one of those dead soppy black and white ones with Marilyn Monroe in it. I think she was dead glamorous Marilyn, just like Madonna and I'm always day-dreaming that I look just like her. Anyway I'd just settled down to watch it when DD walks in. He comes and sit right up close so I was squashed in the side of the settee and starts talking about how Mum was useless now she had Ian. He was smelling like he'd been down the pub and he had two four-packs of Tennants lager so I just decided to ignore him and keep watching telly.

DD wasn't having that though, and he just starts touching me up and pretends he don't hear when I told him to behave. Then I was getting real scared and smacked him one. DD grabbed my hair and starts right in on me, just hitting me, and ripping my clothes and pinching, and he was sort of pinning me down and I got sort of scared and just kicks him hard, you know, where it hurt most, and then I just took off out of there.

I didn't really know what to do and then I remembered what Shaz told me about what the social worker said; you know, about getting accommodated. I was dead scared about going down Social Services on me own, but I was too embarrassed to go round by Shaz's house.

It wasn't half as bad as Shaz had made out, and the woman I saw was dead nice. But she just kept saying she couldn't get me somewhere to live unless Mum wanted that cos I wasn't sixteen yet. She kept asking me questions about why I wanted to get away from home, and I just kept saying that Mum didn't have no time for me. I was too shame to tell her about DD and when she asked me about the bruise on my face I just told her the same story about not paying attention and walking into a lamp-post. Than she tried to tell me that I was better off at home anyway and wanted to come round to the flat with me to try and patch things up. That's when I had to tell her about Mum's group thing, but I was still too shame to tell her about DD.

They must have got in touch with Mum at the community centre cos she came down Social Service with our Ian and DD wasn't with her like I was expecting. When she first come in, I thought she looked ever so worried, and I was even thinking she might kick DD out of ours if I told her what happened. Then the social worker up and tell her all what I said about us not getting on, and starts asking Mum if she was having trouble coping with me. Mum's face just went sort of stiff and she looked like she was ever so mad. She gave me ever such a bad look and starts telling the woman I was only saying that to cause trouble cos I was jealous that she'd had Ian.

The social worker wanted to leave us alone to try and sort things out, but Mum wouldn't hear of it. I guess that's why I got so stroppy. All that time I'd been trying to tell Mum about DD and she'd never wanted to listen. I was fed up with coming second to her boyfriends. I suppose that's why I told the social worker about DD and what he had been trying to do, why I had to come down there.

Mum looked dead embarrassed, then she got angry with the social worker and said she'd put me up to saying it. She said I was a jealous little toad who was always lying to get attention, and that like as not I'd thrown myself at DD like he was always complaining.

I could see the social worker wanted to believe her, and by then I was regretting going down there in the first place. Anyway I didn't like the sound of being accommodated any more, and I figured that DD was already fed up with Mum anyway, so he'd probably get another girlfriend and move out of ours soon enough.

Mum wasn't having that though, said if I hated her so much I might as well stay with the social worker cos she didn't want nothing else to do with me. I kept thinking she'd change her mind, but she just signs these forms the social worker filled in, then stomped off with our Ian. That's how comes I'm in this grotty place now, the social worker said they couldn't find anywhere else to put me.

It's horrible here, most of the other kids was in care and they come here until they get their own flat. None of them want to talk to me and some of the girls been nicking stuff down the shopping centre. There is three women working here most of the time, and some other people that might come for a couple of weeks and then just go. Is like you just don't know who's going to be in charge from one day to the next.

I'm dead fed-up cos the kids pair up and take turns to cook and none of the others want me with them cos they're all better at it than me. They're ever so greedy, just grab everything the minute it get on the table and there's never enough left for me. I've lost quite a bit of weight but I'm so spotty even I can't look at myself.

I cry a lot these days, just cos I don't want to be here and Mum don't want me any more. Dismal Dennis left her about a month ago and when my social worker told me, I went round to see if we could patch things up. Mum reckons it's my fault he's gone. She's happier with just her and our Ian and I guess she figure it'll be too much trouble having me back. My social worker says to give her time, but she don't know Mum like I do. From she decide she's better off without you, she ain't never going to have you back.

My social worker say I'm probably better off out of home if Mum don't want me, but what does she know? At least Mum had time for me when she didn't have a boyfriend . . . and anyway she's Mum isn't it? She'd notice when I was up to anything and she'd talk to me, even if it was just yelling cos I'd done something wrong.

The people in charge here don't care. If you try and ask them for help they just say you have to get on with it yourself cos when you're out of here you won't have nobody to tell you what to do. I suppose being here is just a job to them. I bet they never tell *their* kids to just get on with it.

It's my birthday next week and my social worker says she's coming to take me down McDonald's. I've been there lots of times now, but it's not the same as when I used to go with Mum. *She*'s only coming cos that's what she's paid to do and cos school's been on at her again about me bunking off. I don't know why she don't give it up. Every time she has a go at me I just promise I'll go back to shut her up; but with everybody knowing about me getting chucked out of home I ain't never going back.

Talking about school, I saw some girls from there down the town last week and they told me that Shaz was going round with them now. They said Mum kicked me out cos I fancied her boyfriend. I didn't say anything though. I suppose I'm sort of used to them taking the mick, but deep down it really hurt and I expect that's why I just can't go to school no more.

My social worker's got two kids, a little girl and a boy about my age. I saw their pictures in her purse. She told me their names but I forgot them. They look different from me, happy like. I suppose they never had to go to McDonald's for their birthday. I bet they have a party with all their friends and a cake with candles and all sorts.

Sitting in this crummy room by myself, I really feel like nobody wants to know. I used to think I had it bad when I was living at home, but that was nothing to this. If Mum said she'd have me back I'd be round there like a shot. Mind you, I suppose I could try it on and see what she makes of it.

Yes, I think I might just do that. I'll use my birthday money and get Mum a present – something dead posh. I could even buy a cake and get some candles and take them round . . . surprise her like. That way if she don't let me stay I'll still have

my birthday cake and my social worker is bound to be off
home time I get back here.

Joan Riley was born in St Mary, Jamaica and now lives in Britain.
Her work includes four novels, published by The Women's Press: *The
Unbelonging* (1985), *Waiting in the Twilight* (1987), *Romance* (1988)
and *A Kindness to the Children* (1992).

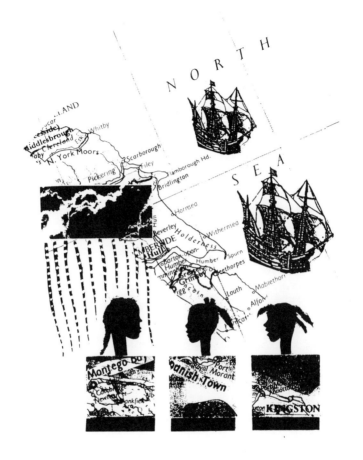

Invisible Mass
of the Back Row

Claudette Williams

Invisible Mass of the Back Row

I stand in the middle of the room, surrounded by anxious faces. It is my turn to recite the day's lesson. The Inspector's ruler points to me.

'Stand up. Recite the adventures of Columbus. What was the date of Columbus' landing in Jamaica? What were the names of his ships? Why was he in the Caribbean?'

My heart pounds. The heat of the morning sun, soaking through the galvanised roof, is magnified inside the schoolroom. The stench of fear is in everyone's nostrils. Something tells me that my days of being hidden, disposed of, dispatched to the invisibility of the back row, are numbered.

I stand up, my limbs shaking uncontrollably, sweat dripping from my armpits, my eyes inflamed. My belly aches. I am petrified. Words fail to come out. They are formed in my head, but my lips do not speak them. The Inspector's eyes pierce me through. They demand a response, demand to be respected and obeyed.

'What was Columbus doing here anyway?' The trapped words inside my head tumble out. The rebel inside me is alive.

The schoolroom becomes even quieter, if that is possible.

'You in for it,' Patricia, sitting next to where I stand shaking, mutters without moving her lips. I know she is speaking the truth.

The Inspector's face is frozen. Miss Henderson, form six teacher, pounces with the ruler. Her face says that she is sure she could not have heard what she thought she heard.

'What did you say, Hortense?'

From I don't know where, a power surges through me. My fists clench. My teeth lock into each other. Miss Henderson reads challenge in my face. I stand still, not daring to say any more. 'What did you say?' she commands, challenging me to dare to repeat my *facetiness*. And again it happens. Words gush out of my mouth. 'Is what Columbus did want? Who invite him here?'

Before the last word has left my lips, the sharp sting of the ruler cracks my knuckles. Stupidly, I had left my clenched fist on the desk in front of me. The blow brings me back to the steam bath. Sweat now drips from my face, floods my armpits, drips from between my legs.

I could kill this woman with her sharp pointed nose, mean eyes and frightened face. We cross eyes, and for an instant I see the fear which has trapped us in this rank, smelly room. Miss Henderson is afraid. She is as much afraid of the Inspector as I am.

My brains, what brains I have left, are bouncing around inside my skull, goading me on. I will get more of the ruler. It is written across Miss Henderson's wrinkled forehead. My life is at an end! At least in this school. If Miss Henderson does not kill me with this ruler, my aunt is sure to finish me off when she hears how I back-chat the Inspector and Teacher Henderson.

My parents are in England and living with my aunt is like walking a tight-rope. One little slip and I am in big trouble. Dis look and smell like big trouble to me.

The lunch bell echoes throughout the school. My salvation? For now, anyway.

Hungry bellies rumble in the steam bath, but we are still transfixed by the Inspector, paralysed by Miss Henderson's stare. Feet shuffle, fingers scratch prickly skin. From outside, there is the freedom of released bodies bouncing against the partition and liberated voices rising. They magnify our imprisonment. But the walls have been breached. The jailers are quick to realise that this battle is lost. For now.

'Class dismissed,' the Inspector grudgingly commands. Miss Henderson lowers her eyes.

'Good afternoon, Inspector. Good afternoon, Miss Henderson,' we recite. Miss Henderson steps aside, stiffly. Fifty tense bodies scurry past, politely, straining to taste the fresh, if hot air of the noon-day world and feed themselves from the lunch women under the cotton tree. But first there is Lorna

Phillips to take care of. Somebody has to pay for this.

'Yo red pickney always sit a de front of de class. Unno t'ink is because yu pretty'. Is only 'cause teacher frighten fi yu pupa,' I curse Lorna, as we bundle down the steps, out of earshot of Miss Henderson and the Inspector.

'Is 'cause yu black and stupid why teacher meck yu sit a de back all de time,' Lorna chirps in.

'Is who you calling stupid? Yo want yu bloody nose right here?'

This is always the outcome of a tense morning in school. A fight often follows the Inspector's visits.

Lorna pushes past me and tries to make a break for the school gate. But I give chase, followed by Samuel, Tim, Patricia, Maud and Yvonne. Today she will pay for being teacher's favourite, for being 'red', for being rich, for having everything I don't have.

'Look how fast she moving on dem marga foot,' taunts Yvonne.

'Come, let we beat her up,' I shout, and we surge forward, pursuing Lorna out of the school.

I might not know the answers, but I can fight.

Just then, from behind the school gate, Teacher Edwards comes into view. He is big, sturdy and beautifully dark, with a baby moustache. He is handsomely dressed in his Dashiki suit. There is a kindness about this man that is not usually found among teachers. He would always listen to you, and not just take the teacher's side. He only beat you if he really feel you was out of order, rude, or you get catch with something you thief. We respected and even liked him.

The running stops, slows to a polite walk. The hot pursuit melts into fixed grins and prim steps.

'Good afternoon, children.'

'Good afternoon, Teacher Edwards,' we still the vengeance in our voices long enough to chant in unison.

Lorna makes the most of Teacher Edwards' presence. Walking as fast as she could, she says her polite good afternoon and makes a beeline for the hill which distances her from the rest of us. She is safe this time. We turn down the hill.

'Meck she gone. We'll get her tomorrow,' we plot. My voice and limbs quiet down. For the first time that day, my heartbeat falls back into its normal silent rhythm. There is always tomorrow.

It is the pain of the Inspector that has fuelled my blood; the pain of the ruler was nothing. Chu, mi use to beatings. One little ruler slap a nothing. But dat renking, facety man. A way him come from? Dis warra warra man, jus' a bother people head. Him' now de score. After all him is suppose to be black.

My uncle say all a dem collude to humiliate, not just me, but all a we, all de people who look like me. All de poor black people dem. Meck him no pick pan de red pickney dem, a meck him t'ink say is we alone no know nothing.

I walk silently down the hill with the others. Each of us is distracted by our own thoughts and anger at the morning. Food hunger is temporarily forgotten. Lorna Phillips and de Inspector dem all de same. Have plenty money and hate we.

At the bottom of the hill, we are nourished by a wealth of warm, familiar sights and smells. The lunch women come into view. They are always there, big and strong, jutting out from the base of the towering cotton tree. Miss Ivy, as always, has on her red tie-head. In the afternoon sun, as she sits on her three-legged stool, it makes her face glow. Her food box is secured between her legs.

Aunt Dine always smells of cinnamon. You know her smell, because if you dare to make her laugh and expose her bare toothless black gums, in quiet moments she will give you a big smothering hug. Her missing teeth give her face a funny, quaint look. She is never scary to us because she lives in our district and we know her.

Miss Mavis always sits to the right of Aunt Dine, because, she says, she is practising to be on the right hand side of her Maker. Miss Mavis has the most beautifully oiled, ivory coloured skin in the whole world, and white, white eyes which twinkle and wink at you when she talks. She is never cross for long, but will cuss you out one minute and tell you scriptures the next. Her face is electric, whirling and changing as she speaks. Her eyes search your face for understanding.

And then there is one-foot Herby who is always late with his sky-juice and snowball. He can argue, always on about 'de damn hot sun', which is 'good for nothing, and only melting him ice, quick, quick, o'clock'.

The boxes are unwrapped. Our senses are assaulted by saltfish fritters, fried dumplings, red herring, cornmeal pudding, sweet potato pudding, oranges, plums, mangoes or sugar-cane, snowball and sky-juice. Smells mingle and whirl, creating a comfortable oasis under the gigantic cotton tree. That same tree serves as a lover's nest and gambling spot at nights. If trees could talk, what stories this one would tell!

We go down the hill. The gloom of humiliation, the pain of the assault on all of us, lifts. We search for our lunch money and think of food. Like swarming bees we descend, shouting our orders to the lunch women.

'Unny stop de noise and wait. How many han' yu t'ink we have?' Miss Mavis quietly reprimands.

The shouts subside only for a moment as we change our orders and surge again.

'Two penny worth of dumpling and saltfish, please Miss Mavis.'

'Mi only want one fritters.'

'Mi jus' want a piece a cornmeal pudding today.'

'But Aunt Dine dat red herring so little bit.'

'Yu have no crackers again Miss Ivy?'

'Ho' come Herby teck so long fi share de ice?'

The clutter and bustle carry on until the sweat is running down the women's faces. Wash-rags, carried on shoulders like a uniform, mop brows, as they try to keep track of orders and change.

'Lord unny pickney is somet'ing else. Unny gone like nobody no feed unny. Dem mus' a wok unny hard a school today.'

The chatter waves and heaves. The banter and retort goes backwards and forwards until the lunch money secured in pockets and knotted in handkerchiefs has been spent for the day.

Boxes are empty. We mingle, swap and taste each others' purchases, eat, talk with mouths full. As we drift away, so do Aunt Mavis, Aunt Dine and Miss Ivy. Herby is the last to pack up and vacate the cotton tree. The forces have been spent for today.

Will I one day move from the back row? Would I be let off from reciting the day's lesson, because I know it, just once? Would it ever be my turn to sit at the front, and not have to answer the Inspector's questions?

The house is buzzing. A letter and a big, big parcel have arrived from England. 'Me mother sending for we. Me and me two brothers going to England.' I sang, 'Me a go a Englan'. Me mumma and puppa send fi we.' Dat will show Lorna Phillips. She have no people in a Englan'. Columbus can get lost. No more standing up in the middle of the class. No more hot, sweaty classroom. No more Teacher Henderson. No more Inspector. Me a go a Englan'.

November sixteenth. It is dark outside. Night creatures are going to sleep. Day animals still don't know it is time to wake up. Inside, the lamp is lit, casting its honey glow on our faces, still dazed with sleep.

'Unno go wash, and put on unno clothes,' Salna orders. Sleepily, we obey.

The sun is creeping over Easington hills, reflecting the honey glow inside. Its full power is still waiting to wake up. I cannot drink any tea, cannot eat what is to be my last piece of hard-dough bread and butter. My stomach is tight. My jaws are refusing to chew on this familiar taste.

'If yu don't want de tea, lef' it an go put on yu clothes. Dem all dey pon de chair, and don't mess up de hair,' I am ordered again. I do as I am told. No time for back-chatting.
Now there is much coming and going. In the dim light of

morning, not yet fully awake, neighbours come to say farewell. They bring small parting gifts of mangoes, and presents for relatives in England, not seen or heard from in many years.

Like a stranger, I greet my new clothes, gingerly feeling, inhaling the new cloth smells. I try to work out which piece to put on first without disturbing my newly crafted hairstyle.

I dress in silence, only now beginning to fully realise. Today, my every action, in this dim morning light, is to be registered in the cosmos as my last in this familiar, tiny, two-roomed house.

We pile into the van just as the morning sun claims its place in the sky. It releases its passions and burns away the last stillness of the night. The silence of parting quiets the most active tongue. The drive to the airport is long and hot. Still, the pain of parting traps us in our silent world.

Who will look after Cousy's grave? Who will make sure that the weeds do not choke her roses?

Cousy had not moved, as she always did, when the sun peeped over the hill top. Had not roused me to do my morning chores when night kiss morning awake. I thought Cousy's coldness was just the passing of night. So I slept on, not noticing that her 'old bones', as she often referred to herself, had not stirred, that her limbs were stiff, that she got colder as the morning got warmer.

Lloyd banging on the door, ordering me to get up and come feed de chickens, alerted the yard. I woke to find Cousy's gentle face tight and still, a trickle of tears running from her opened eyes.

'Why are you crying Cousy?' I asked as I crept sleepily out of bed. There was no reply. And I found myself crying too. Her stillness, her unfocused stare, signalled a change.

I opened the door to find the whole yard gathered outside, waiting. They understood the signals. Death had crept under the door and taken Cousy away in her sleep.

'I want Cousy,' I hollered, as I fell into Miss Olive's arms. Does this mean I won't ever again share Cousy's bed and snuggle into her warm bosom? Won't smell her old mysterious smells, and watch her crinkled face?

Now, this thought forces out the hot salty tears which well up inside. I am leaving her behind. The tears flow freely, soiling my newly polished face. Bringing me back to the speeding van taking me away from Heartease, from Cousy, from my goats, from Lorna Phillips. Towards . . . the gigantic, shimmering aeroplanes.

The sun releases all its enormous strength. The sea retaliates. It shimmers its bluest blue, a blue that envelops the airport and the parked aeroplanes.

The following hours are filled with a numbness. The only parallels I can think of are visits to the dentist with anaesthetic injected to deaden the pain or when you freshly buck your toe on a big rock stone. My inside is dead. I am cold in the blazing sunshine.

Now, everybody is crying, some pretending that they aren't. Handkerchiefs flap goodbye and wipe streaming eyes. My brothers and I are ceremoniously handed over to a pretty, chocolate-coloured woman dressed in a blue uniform. We follow her, reluctantly, into places of strangeness, places with strange lights and strange demands. People smile knowingly and gather up our belongings.

Then we are sitting in the belly of the gigantic metal bird, which we have only seen before from the ground, looking upwards. This is it. We are going to England.

England brings my mother and father back to me. It drags them forward from the fragile recesses of my young memory. I remember snippets of incidents which had told me of their existence. How long have we been separated? Well, it is hard to know. It was hard, those days long ago, to understand what was going on. I cannot count how many days I was without my father's company, nor am I positive of the many years without my mother's embrace. But memory surges suggest seven years, perhaps, without father and five without mother.

I was not to know then, that although I would return many times, that first departure was the beginning of my exile from Heartease.

> Paraffin heaters
> smell
> always just coming
> into cold dark
> places
> afraid and
> excited at the same
> time
> cold
> smell
> wanting to be elsewhere
> in fact Jamaica

'Yes, Salna,' I replied for the tenth time, to my mother's call from the kitchen. A pokey, steamy place at the back of a cold, cold house.

All the houses I see are stuck together, with no place to play outside, no yard. Do children not play outside in this England? Is it always so cold? Does it ever get warm? Does the sun shine here?

'Now listen to me, child,' my mother's dark, youthful face smiles down at me, brings me back to the steamy space. I sit huddled in strange clothes, close to the paraffin heater. 'You had better decide what you are going to call me. You can choose from Mother, Mummy, Mum. The same goes for your father. You've got Dad, Daddy or Father to choose from.'

This little talk put an end to days of nervous tension about deciding what to call my England parents. Having arrived, what do you call these newly acquired people? I dreaded answering my mother's call. What do you answer when strangers call to you, but they are not strangers really, they are your mother and father? I fell back on old responses, familiar language.

No one told me I would need a new language in dis England.

'My mother who dey a England; my mother who a send fa me in a England.' Here I was without a language to reply to her calls. Lorna Phillips, I still hate you, but oh I wish you were here. At least I know your name.

Mum came with me for my interview at Devon Spencer School. She sat right next to me as I read for the Headmistress. I read but did not know the words of this new language, could not read the words of this strange book. I did my best. I read until I was told to stop, being corrected by the Headmistress. The Headmistress was impressed. I was impressed. My Mum was impressed. My impressive reading enrolled me in one five, the hottest, baddest stream in the first year, only second to one six, the remedial stream.

My strategic location in one five has a familiar feel about it. There is no Lorna Phillips. In this group we have all recently arrived, from one island or another but mostly from Jamaica and all poor, clearly black and one rung from the back row, the bottom stream. This is home away from home. I simply settle down to school life and cultivate the culture of the back row. We graduate in hair plaiting, make-up and cussing. Our section of the common-room is dominated by the smell of hair pomander, face powder and Woolworth's latest perfume fragrances.

'You know say Columbus enslave de Indian him fine in the islands. De same one dem who save him life, and help him restock him ships and tell him say him no reach India yet.' Joycelin is feeding us information as she leafs through her latest book, discovered at the local library.

'You lie!' The challenge comes from Fay Green. 'Because is Africans dem enslave and ship to de islands, to slave on sugar plantations, fi make sugar fi white people tea in a England.'

The hair on the back of my neck stands up. The room is suddenly very hot. This man, Columbus, keeps coming back to haunt me.

'With all de tea dem drink in dis place, is we still a fi meck sugar fi dem fi sweeten it,' says Joycelin as she continues to leaf through the book, stopping every so often to throw out morsels about the exploits of slavers, life on plantations and the fights slaves and the indigenous Indians waged for their freedom. Conversations weave and heave. We move back and forth between anger, total disbelief and downright outrage.

'Is who write dat book you reading? Cause is foolishness you telling me. I don't believe a word of it.' Fay Green finally bursts out.

Each new piece of information is challenged and questioned. We discover heroes, rebels, guerrilla fighters. They help us assert our right to be. Toussaint L'Ouverture, Sojourner Truth, Nanny, Cudjoe, Paul Bogle. The books tell us they all come from our own back yard. Thoughts of them mingle with the hair oils, face powder, and self-affirmation lessons which claim space in our section of the common-room.

Group humiliation replaces individual humiliation here in England schools. This bottom from remedial class gets the meanest, most feared teachers in the schools. Their sole intention seems to be to ensure that we know and keep our place. And Columbus keeps coming up. Today's lesson is to make sure we have learnt the lesson of conquest.

Things mingle and whirl in my mind. Easington heat. Easington sweat. English cold. English ice. Frozen faces, frozen information, frozen places.

'Why did Columbus sail to the Indies in 1493, Hortense?' The frozen face cracks momentarily. 'And while you are thinking of the answer, Fay Green you can be thinking of the commodities which Hawkins traded with the Portuguese of the Gold Coast of Africa.'

Indignantly, the back row comes into its own. 'Columbus was looking for a new route to India, so that when he landed in the Caribbean he was good and lost; he thought he was in India. The people who befriended him were massacred and the rest enslaved to mine gold and cultivate sugar. When they died from diseases Europeans brought to the islands, they were replaced by Africans stolen from the Gold Coast of Africa, Miss.'

I said all of this slowly, so that I would say it well. Some of it came out just as I had read it in a book that one of the others had taken from the local library. Slowly, but quickly, because my head was hot and heavy. I can feel the others in the back row feeling proud. We watch the frozen face thaw out. We watch her eyes travel right along the two rows at the back. We watch a stream of red blood rush from the neck to the top of her head.

Fay Green cannot hold her voice back. 'Hawkins traded trinkets for black African people, who were enslaved and shipped to the Caribbean to slave on cane plantations, to make sugar for English people's tea, Miss.'

All eyes are on the teacher. The back row is tense, wanting an explosion.

The school pips signal the end of the lesson and class five, unusually dignified, stands up and leaves the room. Miss remains fixed to her chair.

Whoops and slaps are heard down the corridor. The back row claims a victory. 'She won't be asking us those stupid questions again, will she?'

Voices are raised, claiming, proclaiming, learning the new language in dis here England.

Claudette Williams was born in St Thomas, Jamaica. She now lives in London and is a Senior Lecturer at the University of North London. At the University, she has co-written a series of science activity books for early learners, *Let's Explore Science* (Dorling-Kindersley, 1993/4). Claudette Williams has contributed to a number of anthologies: *Turning the Tables Recipes and Reflexions from Women* (Sheba Press, 1987), *Charting the Journey* (Sheba Press, 1988) and *Inside Babylon* (Verso Books, 1993).

Yemar

Lemn Sisay

Yemar

The world had grown around her like the elephant grass that spurts upwards after the rain season. Here, the elephant grass was made of concrete. The world had sprung upon her like the nightmare of a young child waking and realising that she is still in it. Here was the story that nudged her into the room where the paintings are on fire and Yusuf sits in a purple blazing armchair. The world had entered her and left her in pieces. It had torn down the curtains, smashed the windows and let the storm rush through her. And all she could do was grip the floor for dear life as it shook. All she could do was dig her nails into the carpet and pray, pray that the floor would not split in two and engulf her, lacerating her skin as she falls bounding from the rocks into the centre of the earth, into the centre of herself.

She had seen, touched and felt the beast. She could still smell its breath. Its tongue had burned her skin and left deep scars. The moaning had split the ends of her hair and ricocheted between her temples. He was from deep under the ground and he swirled around her head in the aftermath of his visit. Only her Amharic tongue could scream blue murder. No second language taught words for this. In his wake he had left her a son.

Many tormented thoughts had passed through this room, and if dust were the residue of torment this room had proof. Selborne Social Services Open 6 days a week call 987 2345 office hours and 554 7789 for the duty social worker at any other time. The plaque didn't consider the sobbing mothers, the runaway children, the lost grandfathers and the abused daughter who would be standing shoulder slumped and helpless in front of it, some with too many tears in their eyes to read. The flat grey plaque with thin white ingrained lines for type was from the council department that did the same signs for prisons as for old people's homes, for mental institutions as for children's homes. But she was not to know this.

This country had more signs than most. It needed more direction than her home country. The receptionist was the living body of the plaque. The plaque had become human and sat staring at Yemar over her glasses and through the glass. The regulatory polite smile was given. The forms to fill in. Yemar obliged, handed them in and sat in the waiting room. She caught the glances and the up and down looks from the receptionist through a mirror hanging on the wall by her right side. A sharp draught that felt as if two cold hands were grasping her ankles brought her to the edge of tears. 'How to make your man – make your life.'

The magazines lazily sprawled on the table top offered advice. Her mind pulsed with the words. How to make your man make a mess. How a man makes a mess out of your life how a man makes . . . God made man in his own . . . man makes man . . . how to make a man make a man . . . how to make your man make your life. One silver tear flipped off her eyelashes and fell in her lap. She jerked her head upwards. Took a sidelong glance into the mirror. The receptionist averted her eyes and shuffled some papers.

Yemar flicked through the magazine. She could hear Yusuf's laughter and his grunts. How to make your man make your life. The receptionist walked from her office and through the door with the sign. Assuming the pity posture, she sat on the chair next to Yemar.

'He won't be a minute . . . ' She passed Yemar a steaming cup of sugared tea. It was as if she was speaking to someone on the other side of the road, as if she couldn't see Yemar but through a distance. 'I said he won't be a minute, OK?'

'Thank you,' whispered Yemar, concerned that her voice should be clear and precise enough for the kind lady to understand that she could speak. The receptionist raised her eyebrows in surprise, patted her skirt and tottered back to her former position.

Waiting was all Yemar did not need. Waiting comes after ordeals. Children wait in hospitals. A robber leaves his victims waiting for the police to arrive. But by now Yemar had waited long enough to pass through the grief and learn to live with it. She had drifted as she used to as a child, into a cross between deep thought and meditation. It had been a long time since that had last happened.

The receptionist was frantically banging on her window. It was as if there was another world that she lived in, a whole empire behind that glass. Those who sat in the reception room were the undeserving who wanted desperately to take over her domain. Yemar was doing this. The status quo had been broken by a sleeping woman. Just as the receptionist was about to stand and leave her castle Yemar awoke. The truth is that she hadn't slept properly for the past six months.

'Yes?'

'Mr Goldthorpe will see you now Mrs . . . '

Yemar raised her hand, walked to the reception and passed the lady her cup. 'Many thanks for the wonderful tea,' she said, suddenly finding complete composure. As she was walking towards Mr Goldthorpe's office she turned. 'I hope you don't mind me saying my name is pronounced Fumer and spelt FUMIR.'

'Yes,' answered the receptionist. Her voice sounded surprised, uncertain.

Yemar had spent a long time in hospital and about two years in the country. She had learned that with all the most genuine intent in the world some people simply do not want to know how to say or spell your name, even if they have to use it. She had long taken pride in her name as African, Ethiopian, although many of the African students were named Pleasance or Peace or Horatio. There were some parts of Africa where, at school, you couldn't even mention your African name. You had to have an English name and if you were caught using your African name you would be punished. But Yemar had always liked her name and had grown stronger just spelling and pronouncing it when people were uncomfortable with it.

'Hallo Miss . . . ' He nervously glanced at his papers, 'Miss Yeamashee.'

'Sorry . . . '

'Pardon . . . '

'It's Miss Fumir. Yemarshet Fumir and it's spelt FUMIR.'

'Yes. Yes. Well, I'm not used to the name. I'm sure you'll understand, Miss Fumir.' The social worker smiled the regulation smile. 'Would you like to explain what you need from us?'

Yemar was silent. How would she tell him? He didn't even want to know her name. But he must do something.

How would she let him know that what had happened was so serious that he must find a way to do something? Yemar opened her mouth to speak. She felt the distance from him, the remoteness. As if again she was standing far away from him, making him squint to see and bend forward to listen. If she was as still as stone what difference would it make to him? Would he realise she hadn't spoken? She wrung her hands in her lap. All her nervous energy was in her hands. It was as if she was keeping five baby snakes from falling on the floor, without letting the social worker notice.

Yemar wrung her hands again. Yusuf lay on the table, a grown man dangling his feet from one end and his head from the other end and turning to her in mockery. She stared from him to Mr Goldthorpe. How could she tell him? Who would believe her if they couldn't even be bothered to spell her name right? After all, she had never gone to the police. She hadn't told anyone. She's a good-looking woman. She hasn't even got a family. She'd be in the papers. They'd spit on her, they'd drag her through the streets by her hair. No . . . no she couldn't tell him. She couldn't.

Mr Goldthorpe spoke slowly. 'What do you need? We can't help you if you don't tell us.' The snakes were still writhing in her hands.

'What I need is for someone to look after my baby while . . . you see I cannot afford to keep him. I work night and day to pay for the college, to buy books and even that money cannot pay for a baby and that is the only reason why I am here. To study. I shouldn't have done what . . . I shouldn't have . . . I have made a mistake. I don't know. I hope the Lord . . . What you need, Mr Goldthorpe, what I need is someone to take care of my child until I return to Africa when I can take him home where my family is. You see there I could afford to keep him. It is only that I am here with no family, no home, you see.

'I see,' Mr Goldthorpe scribbled some notes. 'And the father?'

'The man has gone.' The snakes were still. Watching.

'Gone?' He raised his eyes from the paper.

'Yes.' And Yemar was whispering. Her eyes darted back to the floor. And the tears would not stay back behind her lids.

'Here.' Mr Goldthorpe passed a tissue. He looked long and hard at Yemar as she wiped the tears from her eyes. You wipe tears and they disappear. If they come again you wipe them away again. She wished she could do the same with her life at the moment. Wipe it clean with a clean white handkerchief and then get on with doing things properly.

'Yes; he has gone. Disappeared. Left me.' The snakes were moving again. 'I wouldn't want him anyway. My father is ill in Nigeria. I can't even afford the money to visit him. I have the course to finish, Mr Goldthorpe . . . ' The snakes kept writhing, but they never fell to the floor.

'Why would . . . How could any mother leave her child? She must have hated it, the selfish woman,' whispered Sally on the way to church. God had directed this child away from evil and into their hands, safe from the perils of Africa . . . of Africa and a mother who could do no good. Who knows what she would do to it?

It would be wrong to leave him in the hospital. You see? That's just it. Nobody would take him. They'd look. Oh, yes, they'd look but no one would take him . . . but kindness and God's love can help him.

Sally always got through to Paul that bit more just before he went to the church. Indeed this child would have a life with the Lord assured. There was not much choice in the matter – clearly this was the Lord's work. They were convinced. And though problems were foreseeable, God moved mountains and Jesus would help them through. The guest minister's words were so apt. Today God had to have been speaking through him.

'Love thy neighbour as thou would love thyself,' he shouted, holding the Bible in the air.

'Amen,' said Mr Wilson, lingering on the first syllable.

'Amen,' murmured Paul, patting Sally's hand.

Mr and Mrs Dove were preacher and nurse. Mrs Dove – Sally – knew what she wanted. Her home was undoubtedly her castle. Crosses hung on every wall, like pot plants. No Jesus stretched out across the cross, of course. This house was one of those which remembered that Jesus had risen, was no longer impaled on the cross. There were no watching porcelain cats to be found on her mantelpiece. The front room was for visitors and was never to be touched except when cleaned for visitors. On Sundays, the middle room was lived in but the television was often switched off as the devil works through it and there is no place for the devil in this house. Later, the child, his noise quietened by the orderliness around him, came to imagine skeletons clinging desperately to the insides of the wardrobes, anxious not to upset the neatness of it all.

Sally Dove was the daughter of a Lancashire mother and a Scottish man. She had always taken second place to Ruth, her younger sister, the favourite. Crammed into the large oak cupboard in the empty bedroom upstairs was Catherine, Sally's twin sister, born mentally handicapped and capable of rocking her chair a little. She lived at Winnick, where they visited occasionally. The saving grace to this and more for Sally was the church.

The pillar of burning fire gave them strength. Not only the spirit seemed to inspire but also what actually happened in the church community. Concern with this filled large amounts of her time. Who hadn't turned up and who had. Who had a new car and who hadn't. Who'd fallen by the wayside through lust and displayed a little too much godly inspiration. Even speaking in tongues was a source of gossip. God was always around. The empty cross was a reminder of the absent presence. The boy would become used to hearing love spoken of; used to the movement between the gossip in the front room and the journey to the kettle in the kitchen.

Sally was not liked by her mother. They were too alike, both pretending that the cupboards upstairs were only for old unwanted birthday and Christmas presents. They practised kindness and forgiveness. Was this why the quiet-faced boy with noises in his head came to resent kindness? Why he came to think of kindness as the currency of the Christian market?

There was no bartering with it. Just straight sales. Merits were enthusiastically given by God and the church and if not, grudgingly given by friends and family. When kindness was used, it was a trump card, serving many purposes. It shut up the opposition and strengthened the defence, for there were no attacks here. They fought with love and kindness, God and forgiveness. All in all, kindness was a short-term investment in God. A spiritual hit. A little money to the coloured children, some for the church and kindly advice to the younger church members. The receivers of this currency were simply passages. They were the way to God. But here, here was a long-term investment. A surer passage.

On that day, Mr and Mrs Dove thought that here was a kindness and forgiveness that would satisfy the church, would silence their friends, would satisfy God. After all it is He who would offer the challenge but most of all, most of all, though Sally hated to admit it, it would silence her mother.

Sally was actually gleeful when she conjured up the expression on her mother' face. It would silence her mother. She would hate it, but she would have to follow God's will. Kindness and in this case, perhaps forgiveness. Sally knew this - touché. A white family fostering a black child in these nineteen-sixties! Blacks were rioting in America, were flooding England. Rochdale, where Paul grew up, never used to have any; now there's thousands. The stakes were high. The church rumbled, sending tremors through the pulpit.

'And believe the word of the Lord. We are all God's children,' spouted the guest minister.

'Amen,' said Mr Wilson, in his usual robust way.

'Amen, ' whispered Sally, clutching Paul's hand.

Paul was a thinker, a deep thinker. He was often frustrated by Sally's forthright conclusiveness. But he respected her. She had been through a lot in her life and she had done well. She didn't have time to think. Whereas Paul studied his thoughts, his past, his future, mulled them over and prayed to God about them. Sally was sometimes jealous about his air of spirituality. As if he thought he was closer to God. They both fitted neatly into their respective roles. His mother had recently become a Christian. After he had prayed that God would show a sign to her, a Pentecostal church was built on what could only be described as her doorstep. It was built in a piece of wasteland right in front of her house, literally two or three yards away. At 67 she conceded to God and the family bonded closer. Paul was elated at this watershed miracle. It confirmed him in his belief. Soon his sister-in-law and brother were Christians. There was only one who wasn't – and he had a bar in his house.

After much prayer, Paul decided that the child was a gift from God, could and would go on to university, could and would have the best life, could and would be someone. After all, this was not any child. This was a black child, and although the news about it needing foster parents came from the hospital where Sally worked, it could not be just a coincidence. Nor was the church outside his mother's house a coincidence. Nor was the subsequent knock-on effect to his brother and sister and their families. There must have been a message – after all, their lives were in God's hands. There were no problems with conception, so why were they faced with this? He concluded that it was God's will. Sally had concluded that on the way home from the hospital. But it took Paul weeks. God had moved mysteriously. He had moved them mysteriously. There was nothing more mysterious than an African child left from the tyranny of a hard life. He would probably starve, coming from Ethiopia.

Yemar had received a letter at the college about her father's illness. It was as if Yusuf knew. As if burning her was not enough, he was going to squeeze each last hope and inch of her life from all around her. He had exiled her. He was killing her father – he knew how much she loved him. He controlled her stepmother, who had written and spitefully noted that her father would only have a few weeks to live. The letter had taken one week to arrive. She had finished her exams. The college informed her that she could receive the results in Africa if she wanted to, albeit a little later than everyone else. It was important that she passed, if only to defeat her past and lay a path forward, if only to defeat Yusuf. To hear him cry as she became more successful, to hear him moan and burn at her strength and weep at her feet for forgiveness.

The letter cut her deep. She wept at the thought of her father, then at the thought of her son whom she was about to try to get back. She wept at the thought of Yusuf, who couldn't be called a father. Her tears blotted her stepmother's sprawling writing. Yemar slept with the letter gripped in her fist underneath the pillow. The following day, she called Mr Goldthorpe three times. There was no reply. The next day she telephoned four times. No one answered.

Lemn Sisay was born in England of Ethiopian parentage. He is a poet, playwright and vocalist. He has contributed to several poetry collections. He has two published collections of poetry: *Tender Fingers in a Clenched Fist*, (Bogle–L'Overture Publications, 1988) and *Rebel Without Applause* (Bloodaxe, 1992). His recordings include *Black Vibe* (Bebop Cassettes, 1989) and *Live and Unleashed* (1990).

Karima

Aamer Hosein

Karima

For Janette Turner Hospital
In friendship
You know the borderlines

– Listen brother, she says, you can read Urdu, can't you? I'd like you to read this for me. This picture here, what do the words under it say? The man in it, you know, yes, Naeem, he went from Dhaka to Karachi after the troubles and he's one of our Biharis, his parents were in a camp and look at him now, such a big star, and he sings so beautifully too, I've seen him on television and I always listen to his cassettes. He's coming to Wembley? No, I don't think I could. No, it's just that he looks like my Shahzad.

Karima. She used to work in the food shop opposite. I'd go there late in the evening, tired of thinking or writing, for a pack of cigarettes. I don't know how it began but one night we talked and soon she started coming up to get her letters written. Sometimes to someone in Karachi or Pindi, or sometimes, rarely, to addresses in Dhaka. Her messages were always the same. I'm well, working hard, sorry I can't send more money this time, I can't come home, not this year, how is Bachu? He must have grown so big by now. She didn't have an address, so all mail should be sent to her care of us. And then, at the end, she'd ask for news of Shahzad.

– Shahzad was my son, she says, born when I was still a child. His father was called Badshah. He was hardly older than me. Born in the old country though, in Patna, before they came away – his parents and mine – when the country was divided by the strong ones. I was born in Dhaka. I always knew my Badshah, always knew that I'd marry him. His parents had a shop that sold provisions, but he was a mechanic. Already working hard when I married him, looking after his mother

---

47

and younger brother too. He'd sold his father's business and put the money to good use, to set up on his own. We lived quite well. I didn't have to work, though so many women around me did, and some of our neighbours envied me. In the evenings I'd put on a bright fresh cotton sari and white or red flowers in my hair. Sometimes he'd take me in a rickshaw to the cinema. They'd tease me – unkindly, at times – when my man wasn't around, calling us the royal family because of our good food and our happy faces. In our community no one lived beyond their means but we looked as though we did. And when my son was born I called him Shahzad because I thought a king should have a prince for a son, because I wanted to turn their taunts into blessings, because I wanted him to have a hundred times our luck. His father wanted us to go to Karachi. That's where the real rewards could be had. That was where he should have gone in the first place, he said – that's where they spoke our language, that was the real Pakistan. Those Banglas, he said he couldn't really understand them. We always spoke Urdu at home. He could read and write it, too. But I couldn't really understand him. Perhaps I was too young. And I was born in Dhaka. It was the only place I'd ever known. I could speak Bangla like my own tongue. The people, too, they seemed like my own. But these were matters for men and the old people, who remembered the old country, remembered something better, and told us of what they'd had to sacrifice to brings us to this new land, where we could follow our beliefs in peace, live our lives in peace. But what peace? My boy was two when the troubles came. Perhaps his name had tempted fate, perhaps I shouldn't have been so happy. Perhaps my husband shouldn't have loved his country so much. Because suddenly East Pakistan wasn't going to be his country any more. It was changing names.

Karima. One of those ageless women with figure and features carved from ebony. When she loosened her hair it looked like a black storm-wind. She spoke the rapid Bihari

Urdu of Dhaka but over the years I knew her it acquired an
even more pronounced Bengali intonation and a strong overlay
of English words. How old must she be now? Was she thirty-
three when she first came to see us, all those years ago, when
we helped her with her papers, when her man slapped her, and
all those other times when life became too much for her? Well,
almost – life will never be too much for Karima. I changed
addresses and stopped thinking about her. Life doesn't take me
her way all that often. Anti-Muslim tracts, the BJP, sectarian-
ism and fundamentalism, desolation over the Gulf War, the
computerisation of my writing, failure to read Foucault,
distaste for Derrida and deconstruction, and yet again my
stories hadn't earned me the fare home. No time to spare, to
write letters for Karima. Maya would see her at the shelter
sometimes. She'd bring her man to the community centre twice
a year on Eid, and helped out with the crèche when she wasn't
working in their shop till midnight. But then Maya left the
shelter for a job in the media and life doesn't take her that way
all that often.

Karima. She used to talk so freely she'd shock me some-
times. But there were things she wouldn't talk about. I've seen
too much, she'd say, and fall into silence.

– Brother, don't you ask me to tell you about the camp, she
says, how can you expect me to remember anything about it?
Crowding, filth, hunger, people complaining. We'd lost everything. Later I went out with the other women to sell things in
the city – pencils, feathers, whatever we could lay hands on –
while our men found work in factories, did the jobs that men
in that rich city would never do. They called us refugees. But
how could we be? If the only home we'd ever known had cast
us away because we were suddenly foreigners, how come we
were foreigners here, too, in Pakistan, the country where we
were supposed to belong? Homeless here, homeless there.
Sometimes the shit-stink of those camps still fills my nostrils
and I think of it as the smell of fear.

– Long live Pakistan. He was still shouting those words as he lay dying, my man. Those last terrible days in Dhaka. My boy was two years old. First the Punjabi soldiers had come in from across the sea and begun to pillage around the edges of the city, so people said, and people said that Bengalis and Biharis alike should run for their skins. There were stories of massacres – of students, peasants, passers-by. But Badshah said the soldiers were our friends and they'd come to rescue us from those marauding Banglas. And then even the neighbours to turned on us. They'd loved me, I was young and pretty, shared food with them and didn't mind their teasing. Because I often wore yellow they said I looked like springtime and called me Basanti. But now they'd changed their faces. Dirty Biharis, they said, go home or we'll get you. That day a group of them, so big, all men, turned up. Some of them were the sons of women we knew. Get out, get out, go to your murdering Punjabi masters, they shouted. But we're not harming anyone, this is our home, said my man in Bangla. So say Joy Bangla, Joy Mukti Bahini, one of them said – Victory to Bangladesh and its liberation army. Another one had seen me, cowering in my thin night-sari with the screeching boy in my arms, and he came towards me. Badshah went mad. Out, you Bangla traitors, he said in Urdu. He had a broken bottle in his hand. This is Pakistan. Pakistan Zindabad. I'll live and die in Pakistan. Then die, said the one who'd been ready to attack me, and he set my man on fire. I swear he did. The stench of burning flesh still fills my nostrils. I saw my Badshah burn, still screaming, Long Live Pakistan. He told me to run. At least I think it must have been him. Because those bastards, too, they let me go, and one of them said in Urdu, Take your child and run. And I did. Through the flames of houses dying, past burning bodies, beneath the stars of the sky veiled in the smoke of shame, amid brothers tearing out each others' throats, I ran. To where God took me. He must have been weeping. Or perhaps he had just turned his face away. Who can blame Him if this is what His children do?

– What I remember next is being on that boat to Pakistan.
With my mother-in-law and my husband's brother. Memories
of the camp are blurred, but the city beside it was dry and cold
at night, grey instead of green like green, moist Dhaka where
the sun warms your skin even in winter. Those feelings, fire
and ice, those my bones remember. Of course I never knew
then that my destiny lay in cold cities. All I thought of was my
grief, survival, and when I began to regain my senses I thought
about my child's future. That's why, when Rahim my husband's brother began to look at me with longing in his eyes, I
too began to turn toward him. The women around me – so
many of them knew more about men than I did, they'd tie their
saris tight when they went into the market-place, and wink and
smile at customers – the women around me told me I could do
much worse by myself and Shahzad than a man who was
related to my son by blood. He was younger than me, at least
three years. I remember his calf-eyes, his scabby knees and
dirty feet when I first came to his mother's house as a bride.
Even then he'd bring me gifts of jasmine buds and guavas.
Now, in our new homeland, I saw him for the first time as a
man. We'd seen too much, our ways had changed. Grown old.
And after all, how old was I, barely twenty-one? My man dead,
my boy barely speaking, with only my untrained hands to help
me live? And young blood has its needs, too, you know, sister,
and Rahim my husband's brother was handsome. But I never
would forget my Badshah.

    – So I married again. Of course my mother-in-law wasn't
happy, but at first I thought that my moment of happiness had
brought the sorrow of her son's death back to her. I thought
that having her grandson with her would console her and once
again, in a new city, we'd bring back to her a family and some
fragment of a new life, however fragile. For we were in Karachi
now, a city bigger than I'd ever imagined, with tall tower
blocks and smelly camels and the salt stale smell of the nearby
sea rushing, gushing into our nostrils. My husband's brother,
now my husband, took me to the sea once, by Clifton, you

could ride tin horses on the pier and men in Punjabi clothes
sold salted peanuts in their shells and blond children pulled at
their mothers' skirts. I was happy for an hour but then I started
weeping. I don't know whether it was because I missed
Badshah, who used to take me for walks and on pleasure-trips,
or because the big heavy men around us reminded me of the
Punjabi soldiers I'd seen in Dhaka, or because among all these
strange people I suddenly felt strange, and foreign, and poor.
We were small and thin and dark and the Urdu we spoke was
alien to the people around us. We scarcely made them understand us, even though we thought we were speaking their
language and we understood them quite well. Bengali log, they
called us, but we were Bihari and Pakistani, we thought, even if
we'd never seen Bihar and we were new in Pakistan. And I was
pregnant with Rahim's child, too, and a heavy belly makes me
weep. I don't know why, but I knew that I'd have a boy. When
my second son was born his father called him Habib but in my
heart I called him Badshah after his dead uncle who should
have been his father, and when his grandmother began to
called him Bachu I often wondered whether we shared a secret
name for him, knowing that our lost one had sent us a sign.

– Rahim started work as a chauffeur in a big house in
Defence and as soon as I could get Bachu away from my breast
I began to work in the same house, nannying, ironing, stitching
and looking after the mistress's needs. That went on for years.
My mother-in-law was cruel to me, but most of all she was
cruel to my older boy. She'd go into rages and shout at him,
blaming him for all sorts of things. Her worst outbursts were
when she'd accuse him of having brought ill-fortune to the
family and sucking out his father's life. As if she'd forgotten
that he was two when his father died and it was the big men on
top who'd united and divided countries and set brothers
against each other to tear out each others' throats and their
sisters' wombs. Even today our relatives write to us from
Bangladesh, begging us to send them money, begging us to
send for them, to bring them to Karachi, to Dubai, to London

– anywhere. And Lord, your floods and storms, they respect no one, but love us poor best of all.

– New days of misery had come upon us. Rahim's exhaustion, his sense of not living up to his brother's dreams, his disappointment in the new country where we lived beneath a stairway in two small rooms and shared an outside latrine with other servants from the compound, all served to turn him against the child that was not his son, who reminded him, perhaps, of his older brother, who was one more mouth to feed, clothe and send to school. I'd insisted that Shahzad like his father should learn how to read and write, have a profession, at least live up to his father's memory that way, even if he couldn't go beyond what my dead man had done. We'd always been told that this was the land of money and opportunities, but Rahim felt we only had enough for one child, and that child had to be his son. I felt that Bachu was being taken away from me. I worked all day and the child was looked after by his grandmother. Maji, too, like Rahim, seemed to save all her love for Bachu. She wouldn't feed Shahzad when he came back from school, encouraging him to go up to the kitchen of the big house instead to beg for scraps. So I became even more protective of him, keeping everything for him, my money and my love.

– The boil burst open one day when the children in the big house had a party. They sent for Shahzad, and Maji too went up with Bachu, to keep an eye on the children. Rahim was meant to help serving the fried savouries and sticky cakes and pink pastries while I was in the house, looking after the needs of the fancy ladies. I found out later that Saima, the little miss whose birthday it was, had turned on a big tape-recorder and got all her guests dancing to pop music. At some point she'd called to Shahzad and asked him to dance. Bachu came running to me on his fat legs, telling me to come out and see what was happening there. I went out, into the garden, where the sun was just setting. Surrounded by a circle of clapping, cheering children, Shahzad was wiggling, twisting, his feet rose and fell, the music had him in thrall. Look at your beloved, said his grandmother. Dancing like a whore, like a eunuch. The boy had told me he wanted to be a star, like those men on television in bright jackets or the heroes in the movies with a song and a swinging step for every occasion, but I'd never listened to him, thinking of his words as a child's rambling dreams.

– I grabbed him by the ear and pulled him down to our room. Down there I thrashed him while Maji watched, exulting. It was the first time I'd ever hit him, but as I did I swear that I felt that the hand that struck was not mine but his uncle's, and as I flogged Maji came up for her turn and I slapped her as well with the back of my hand. When Rahim drove the Sahib home from his club that night he found us all crying and screaming, and without asking what had happened he gave Shahzad another few slaps and Bachu a smack, too, for good measure. The next day early, Shahzad was gone, and it was weeks before we had news of him. He'd found a job skivvying for some mechanic. He was twelve years old.

I picked up a book about the failure of Punjab's Green Revolution from a friend's place on Sunday afternoon, and read about the Sikh farmers and how their discontent derived not from religious differences but landlessness and dispossession. Three days later the book's author was on the box, supporting Malaysia's Mahathir in his diatribe against the North's exploitation of the South, while screen images flung Fillipino forms, scavenging in muck heaps, at our faces. The rule of Pepsi-Cola capitalism. The Earth Summit is nigh. Anger's lava boils on both sides. The rich masters of destinies trade insults on behalf of the deprived. The Third World, convenient category, the forfeit. And I was trying to write about homelessness. Doing my research, my intellectual fieldwork. On public platforms, or private white paper in poetry or prose, we trace our trajectories of exile and expatriation, claim landless negativity as the writer's preserve and sing homelessness as the eternal ineradicable condition of the human soul.

*Celebrate the gap between our raw material and our present
situation. With pride we assume the mantle of the dispossessed.
What lies, what postures. So long since I've even thought about
it. I wanted to write something about the Sikh farmers, but I'd
been away too long. The smell of a subjective landscape gone.
Irreducibles reduced to beckoning banalities. No grants or
awards around for homesickness these days. Plan to save the
price of a plane ticket 'home' dissolves in the foggy business of
living. You shouldn't even think of 'home'; it's out of intellectual fashion. Illiterate voices fight the vagaries of a language
too remote to contain them. Polemic is out, the gentle weave of
'fiction' veils the pain that mustn't be spoken. Too loud,
aggressive or sentimental, simply over the top. This ain't no
story, brother, you're overmining the documentary vein; it's
journalism, a tract.*

*I watched the stub-end of a documentary about Green
Revolution Technology in the Punjab, watched a Bihari
farmer, one of the 'Bhaiyyas', economic refugees migrating to
work in the Punjab these days. They don't have their own land
in Bihar, though they have the skill to till the soil for others,
and the money they send back helps the people at home. The
Bhaiyya's tones and mangled verbs brought back the sound of
Karima. Who used to bring me her letters and her questions
and her stories. Bear witness to her, I wrote that night, in
foreign words that she wouldn't understand.*

– It wasn't too bad in those first days in London, brother,
she says. My salary was being paid in rupees back at home,
and a secret part of it went to Shahzad. He'd promised he'd
come home, continue his schooling. It was only for a short
time. The mistress's son had some strange problem, he couldn't
walk or speak properly, and she'd brought him here for treat-
ment. One or two years, and then I'd go back home. The
workload, if anything, was lighter than in Karachi. I slept in
the children's room and could watch two, three Hindi videos in
one day. The food was good. In the afternoon I took the

children to the park, the boy in his push-chair, and I found some other women there. Some of them talked about being like prisoners, how hard their employers made life for them. One or two of them were Bangla. There was also the halal butcher down the road. He was Bangla too, and he told me about the women and men who would come here on one pretext or another and just disappear, into an underworld of sweatshops, restaurants, groceries, earn their living in pounds and send more money home than they'd ever imagined. A hard life, but worth it in the end. It didn't impress me much, then, but what I thought was that somehow I could bring Shahzad here, even if I had to go back he could stay, someone like the Bangla butcher could do with an able-bodied lad like him. He kept on asking me to come and work a few hours in his shop; he said a clever woman would be a help and I could have done with the extra foreign cash, but when I tried to talk to the mistress she wouldn't hear of it and thought I was being ungrateful.

– When I'd been here six months the mistress said my visa was up, I had to go home. I said Sister, if my salary is too much for you to pay you can send me out to work at the neighbours'; you know they could do with an extra hand, or I could do a few hours at the butcher's, maybe Saturday or Sunday. But Karima, she says, I'm going back myself; you know little Baba's so much healthier now, and it's getting cold, and your husband wants you home. You've got your ten-year-old son to think of and your mother-in-law's getting old and very sick. But my other boy, Sister, I said, you know I've been sending him money to go to school – She cut in, Karima, she said, there was an accident . . . your boy . . . a van . . . Rahim . . . When? I said. My feet had turned to sunken rocks. The sockets of my eyes were on fire. Oh . . . six weeks, a month, I think? There didn't seem to be any point . . . Saheb said your people thought it would be better if I didn't tell you, after all you'd find out soon enough at home, and I told him to advance Rahim some money . . . for the . . . you know, the prayers and all . . .

– I kept quiet. What could I say? The stench of burning

flesh, the shit-smell of the camps, the faces of marauders and the scared eyes of the ones who ran, flowed before my eyes. They lived in me. I waited a day. Then I asked for fifteen pounds and an afternoon's leave to buy things for my husband's brother – yes, that's what I called him and the mistress didn't even notice – and my little boy. I left all my things in the flat, took the key with me, and I ran. I walked slowly, proudly, but I ran, the open market was Dhaka on fire, and if I didn't move calmly one side or the other would get me. I made my way to the butcher's shop. His eyes had told me the whole story. I knew I'd have to pay in some way the price of my stay, just a hiding place to start with. At first I was terrified that the mistress would set the immigration people on me because I'd unthinkingly walked away with her key, wanting to go there later to get my stuff, but of course I soon gave up that plan, and no one came after me. Later? I still tremble. That's another story.

– I've been with the butcher seven years now. I stay here alone when he goes to Bangladesh. What if someone recognised me and realised I couldn't be his wife? And how would he explain a strange Bihari wife from London, and what is there for me now in Dhaka? And how could I go with a Bangla man to the city that killed Badshah? But here, we're all the same, Bihari or Bangla. He's only hit me once, when he caught me taking more money from the till than he thought I should for Bachu, because I still send money to the people in Karachi, and always add a little for Shahzad because no one ever wrote from there to tell me that he'd gone. But of course I can't let them have my address – after all, who knows? – Rahim may still remember that he has a wife and somehow turn up here to find me. But maybe the money I send has made him forgive me, if there is anything to forgive. In the end, it's between me and my God. Of course I still think of Bachu, but he never really was mine to start with, and perhaps he's best off with his father. Life isn't any easier here for us, people stare and curse at you on the streets and threaten you in your shop late at night. And the hours are so long. This isn't a good home for our young, when you really think about it.

– When the butcher hit me I packed my stuff and walked off to a place that some Bangla woman had told me about, run by women for other women. Some of them spoke Urdu. I stayed there a few days, then I called the butcher from a coinbox and told him to get me from the post office down the road. All the women said I was crazy to go back with him, but I explained to them that I'd told him, if you ever hit me again I'll cut you to pieces with your own carving knife, and if you don't pay me my proper share of the takings I'll report you for every petty crime under the sun. My words hadn't really been that hard, but I'd said enough to put the fear of God in him and I think he wanted in his way to keep me happy.

– I hate these winters, especially when the butcher's away. Letters from my people are rare, and sometimes I wonder if the money I send there ever gets to them. I long for news of Bachu. I have a photograph of him which Maji sent in some moment of pity, but my greatest regret is that in my haste I forgot to pick up my photographs of Shahzad. Since I lost him I've stopped feeling anything for Pakistan. Some nights I dream of him, talking to me, telling me he didn't really die, that he lives in the television now and sings there. That's why I collect every picture I can of the singer Naeem and paste it in my album. He's slim and strong, his eyes are like rain-clouds, and his skin shines like copper in the sun. I know that's how my boy would have looked if he'd grown to be a man, because that's what his father was like, and Shahzad was just like my Badshah.

––––––––––

Aamer Hussein was born in Karachi, Pakistan. He was educated there and in India. He moved to Britain in the early 1970s and studied History and Languages at the School of Oriental and African Studies (SOAS), University of London. He teaches part-time at SOAS and is also a critic and reviewer who writes regularly for the *Times Literary Supplement*. He has contributed to several fiction anthologies. His own collection, *Mirror to the Sun*, was recently published by Mantra.

The Visit

Merle Collins

The Visit

The woman sat leaning forward. Left elbow on leg, left hand holding up her chin, clamping shut her lips. Not hiding her look of sullen disinterest. From the doorway, her daughter watched her. Took in the droop of the shoulders, the emptiness in the heavy-lidded black eyes.

'You watching that programme?'

Miriam shrugged, not moving her head, not moving her eyes from the television. Catherine sighed, leaned in the doorway and turned her eyes towards the television. *Jensen's Dream!* The woman was trying to prevent Jensen from getting the deal on the plantation. Catherine hoped that he would find out in time to stop her. She glanced over at her mother. Lord! Look at her! She had to choose the most uncomfortable chair in the room, quite in the corner over there! And look at her face! Anybody come in here and see her looking like that must think I making her see trouble! Just look at her! Catherine sucked her teeth and turned away from the doorway, moving back to the kitchen.

Martin looked up from his job of washing dishes at the kitchen sink. He chuckled, stepped back and blocked his sister's path with his elbow. 'Behave yourself, non!' he said in a low voice. 'Leave the lady alone!'

Catherine matched his tone. 'Go and watch her! Go and see how she sit down poor-me-one as if somebody thief she best clean-neck fowl!'

Martin laughed quietly, the sound staying down in his throat. He picked up a glass and placed his hands back in the water. 'Behave yourself,' he repeated, 'leave her alone!'

His answer was a prolonged sucking of teeth as his sister moved towards the refrigerator.

Jensen was confronting his secret adversary. He was beginning to suspect that something not quite right was going on.

Miriam had heard the whispering. Guessed that it had something to do with her. She removed her hand from under her chin, frowned, looked cross-eyed at the door, shifted herself sideways in the chair, crossed her legs and leaned her head cautiously back. Her right ear just touched the cushion.

An advertisement. Some kind of sauce. Miriam didn't hear what sauce it was for. A far-off memory came back to her. An advertisement on radio years ago. 'Don't say Worcester! Say Bee and Digby's!'

Miriam cleared her throat and hunched her shoulders. Couldn't they do something to make it a little warmer? Put on the fire or something? Miriam yawned. She would have liked to go and lie down. Cover up. She smiled. *Kooblay* up! But for sure Catherine would want to know if she was ill or something. Quietly, so as not to be heard, Miriam sucked her teeth and turned in the chair. Her body was curved, head down, her back turned now towards the television.

April in England. Catherine and Martin had said when they wrote it was a good time to come. Not very hot, but good weather. Springtime! Good weather! Well I wouldn't like to see bad one! Last week, when they had gone to visit Cousin Bertrand in Huddersfield, it had snowed! Miriam shivered. Martin, who wasn't a bad child, really . . . Not like his sister. Is as if she think England is hers and she doing me a favour to have me here! Favour? I want to go home, yes! I want to go home where me is woman in me own house!

Martin said that Huddersfield and that whole area around there was like that. Always cold. Always cold. When there was snow in Huddersfield, he said, it didn't mean that there was snow in London, too. In fact afterwards they knew that it hadn't snowed in London that day. But snow or no snow, it well cold! It well, well cold!

I tell you, eh, it hurting me heart. Catherine! Look at Catherine, non! I remember how I nurse that child! Puny, puny, she nearly dead, yes! They didn't even think she would survive! And now acting with me like if she think she is queen!

When she had sat there in Peggy's Whim, high up on the hill above Hermitage, writing Martin and Catherine here in

England, she never would have thought that England was like this. No. 30 Rose Mansions, Bedford Street, London NW . . . NW either 3 or 5, she could never remember. Those England addresses were so long! Rose Mansions! She had expected . . . she had expected . . . well, not a *mansion*, but something different to this. This high, high building, all the markings on the wall downstairs, and you had to travel up in a dark, dark elevator! Like a hole! And even those steps! Miriam lifted her head, turned, looked around her. I mean, when you reach inside here, it not bad. It nice, she conceded. They have the place well put away! Well put away!

Furtively, she looked around the room. The little carpet well nice, the bookcase in the corner well neat, the pictures on the wall, well . . . not my choice, these kind of mix-up colours that you don't even know what you looking at, but is all right. Miriam's eyes moved to the records stacked in the corner, the music set on the side by the television. Everything well put away! Is to be expected. Both of them know from time how to take care of a place. They didn't grow up anyhow, even if self we was poor. Her eyes travelled around the room. She looked down at the corners. The place clean. The place well clean. Catherine could work. I know that. And Martin never had nobody servanting for him. He accustom cooking and looking after himself. He spend enough time looking after the house and seeing after Catherine while I go to work! So they all right. They could see after theyself from time!

But . . . Miriam looked around the roon again, sucked her teeth softly, leaned her head back against the cushion. So this England is place to live too, then? Only coop up, coop up inside a house all the time? Miriam sucked her teeth again, too loudly this time.

'You all right, Mammie?' Catherine asked from the doorway, unbuttoning her jeans at the waist to ease the pressure.

'Yes,' Miriam answered in an almost questioning tone, a resigned sort of tone that infuriated Catherine. 'Yes, I all right, yes.'

'Well, Mammie, how you doing *kabuse, kabuse* so? As if you seeing trouble?' Miriam sniffed, held on to the arms of the chair and drew herself to a more upright position. 'Why you sit down there in the chair looking poor-me-one, poor-me-one so? Lively up yourself, non!'

'Madam Catherine, if you don't want me to sit down in you chair, just tell me, yes. I not beggin nobody for a cup of water, non! I have me house, yes. I didn't ask allyou to come up here. So I could pack me things whenever allyou ready! All I will ask you is to drop me on the airport please. And even self you don't want to do that, I sure I could find me way. I not beggin nobody for a drop of water, non! I could go back home in me house this evening self, self!'

Martin pushed past his sister, walked towards his mother, laughing. 'So who is allyou now?' he asked. 'Who you cursing in smart there?' He sat on the arm of the chair, hugged her, leaned his head against hers.

'You smell of onion, boy! Don't try to mamaguy me at all! Move away from me!'

'Come on, Mums. Don't take things so hard.' He put his other arm around her. Catherine grumbled something and moved back into the kitchen.

'I want to go home, yes,' said Miriam. 'Youall just drop me on the airport let me find me way, please. I don't want to come in people place come and give them trouble!'

'Mum, why you acting as if you with strangers? How you mean in *people* place come and give them trouble? Who is this *people*?'

'I don't have time to bandy words with you and you sister, non! I . . . '

'My sister? You daughter, yes! Come on Mums!' He shook her gently. 'Is just a short holiday. Relax and enjoy yourself. You're so tense up! Is only because Catherine wants to see you happy. You just sit there looking so sad, hardly eating . . . How you think we feel?'

'I not trying to make youall unhappy, so let me go where I

happy, I don't like this place. It cold, cold; you can't move; if it little bit bright, which is hardly, and I want to take a walk outside, I have to say where I going, as if me is some little child; I have to ring doorbell to annoy people for them to let me in again . . . How people could live like that? In a house, in a house all day long?'

'Mums, that's the way it is here. And it's more difficult because we have to be running around, getting Carl to school and to the baby-sitter. We couldn't take our holidays same time, so I have to be rushing off to work sometimes; it's different! But it's just a short holiday! Enjoy yourself! We want to see you feeling happy! And look, you even have a chance to meet your grandson for the first time!'

'That self is another thing. Perhaps you should have send that child home for me since after the mother dead. The two of you letting him do exactly what he want. The child talking to you just as he want, saying what he feel? No. Is not so. Is so England children is, then? No wonder it have so much bad thing happening all over the place!'

Martin removed his arms. Linked his fingers, unlinked them and leaned towards the small table to pick up the remote control for the television.

'You not watching that, non?'

'What?' His mother's eyes followed the direction of his glance. 'No. No. I not watching no television!'

Martin pressed a button on the control. The image faded. 'Carl's all right, Mum. He's doing pretty well at school and . . . I encourage him to express his ideas.' He leaned forward again, put down the control, sat looking at the photograph of his son on the side table. Carl was holding a ball, looking straight into the camera, his tongue out. That had been taken last summer, up on Hampstead Heath. Carl was wearing a T-shirt and shorts. Martin's long face was serious, thoughtful, as he watched his son's laughing face. 'Carl's a fine child, Mums.'

'Papa, take care of allyou children as allyou want, you hear. Is your responsibility. I just want to go where I living!'

'You only have two more weeks, Mum.'

'If you could organise it for me to leave before, I will be very grateful.'

Martin hunched his shoulders. Cracked his fingers. 'Okay,' he said. 'Okay, Mum. Whatever you want.' He sat there a while longer, then stood up and moved back towards the kitchen.

I know he feeling bad, but I just don't like this place! Not me and England at all! After a while, Miriam pushed herself up from the chair and walked slowly out to the kitchen.

'We're almost finished,' Martin said.

'Nothing I could do?' Miriam asked.

Catherine turned from taking something off a shelf. Picked up the jug of juice. 'Just put this juice on the table for me, Mammie. And if you want, while I setting the table, you could take out those clothes in the washing machine and hang them up in the bathroom.'

'All right.'

It had started from the time she reached the airport here, really. Before that, Miriam had been excited about the visit. It was only when she reached Heathrow that she started feeling perhaps she should have stayed at home.

Walking up in that line and waiting to go to one of those customs officers. Was customs, non? Customs, or immigration, or something. One of them. Just standing in that line she had remembered school, all those donkey years ago. Standing in line for the ruler from Teacher Alfred. And that man was a beater! She remembered a day when she hadn't known all of her poem. She could even remember the book! Royal Readers, Book . . . Book . . . She couldn't remember which number Royal Readers, but it was Royal Readers, anyway. And the lesson was:

Lives of great men
All remind us
We can make our lives sublime

And departing leave behind us
Footprints on the sands of time
Footprints that . . .

And that's the part that she had forgotten. Standing in line at Heathrow airport, Miriam realised that she *still* couldn't remember it.

Standing taking clothes out of the washing machine, she didn't remember it still. Miriam laughed at herself, out loud. Said, 'Well yes, wi!' Catherine and Martin exchanged glances.

The man at the airport desk had asked a lot of questions. And Miriam had started to feel guilty. She didn't know why, because she didn't have anything to hide. But she had felt really guilty. It was as if he thought she was lying about something.

'You say your daughter and son invited you here on this holiday?'

Miriam had cleared her throat, put her hand to her mouth, said, 'Sorry!' Inclined her head slightly. 'Yes, sir.'

'And this here; this is the address you're going to?'

'Yes, sir!'

'What does your daughter do?'

'She's a teacher, sir.'

'Your daughter is a teacher in this country?'

He had looked up at her then, lifting his eyebrows questioningly.

So what the hell? You think I can't have a teacher daughter here? 'Yes, sir.'

He kept her waiting while he looked through her passport again. There was nothing to see. She had only travelled to Trinidad on it before. Many times. To sell things in the market there. And to Barbados once. He seemed to examine each stamp. Then he picked up her ticket. Examined that, too.

'Will your daughter be here at the airport to meet you?'

'Yes, sir.'

'You'll be here for three weeks?'

Well look at the flicking ticket, non! 'Yes, sir.'

Finally, he had looked up at her and his eyes seemed to say, 'Well, I guess I'll let you through, even though I'm sure you're lying.' His lips didn't say anything more. He stamped her passport.

By the time Miriam had got through customs and walked out to find Catherine, Martin and Carl, Martin's six-year-old son, waiting for her, she was near to tears. Something that hadn't happened for a long time. Her shoulders were hunched and she was feeling as small as Cousin Milton's little Maria back home; Maria who usually stayed with her in Peggy's Whim.

She had felt strange with her children and grandson from the beginning. She found that she just couldn't laugh and talk with them as usual. Especially when Carl said, '*You're* my nan?' And she started wondering why he had said it like that.

And then she found that Carl wasn't like a child at all. He asked big-people questions, talked all the time, and Catherine and Martin just wouldn't shut him up. That must be England style. They didn't grow like that at all.

And Miriam's voice began to sound strange in her own ears, especially when Carl talked to her in that funny accent of his. It made him sound even more like big people.

Two more weeks away! The second of May. Miriam wondered if Martin would try to get the date changed. She wouldn't say it again, but she hoped that he would remember.

It rained on April the twenty-seventh. They travelled by the underground train. Took a taxi to the station, hurried out in the rain, and went with the two suitcases down the escalator to take the Northern line to King's Cross. Then they changed to the Piccadilly line, which went all the way out to Heathrow airport.

At the BWIA airline counter, Miriam began to brighten up. She smiled often. Even seemed to be holding herself back from exploding with laughter. She touched Carl on the head and said, 'Young Mister Carl, eh!'

'You must come again, Nan,' Carl said

'All right, son.' Miriam laughed, glanced at Catherine.

'You know you're only saying that,' said Catherine, leaning across and straightening her mother's collar. 'You didn't like it at all.'

'Well,' Miriam shrugged, still smiling, 'all places have their people.'

'Yes, Madam Diplomat,' said Martin.

Miriam laughed again, leaning back in the way that they remembered. Martin and Catherine looked at each other and shook their heads. Catherine's smile was disbelieving. 'So Mammie you just start to enjoy yourself, then?' she marvelled.

'Child, leave me alone, non. Is home I going, yes.' Miriam touched her daughter's face. 'Don't mind. Don't mind that!'

'Well I never!' said Catherine.

They sat in the airport cafeteria and drank orange juice. 'This orange juice could have do with a little touch of something stronger in it!' laughed Miriam. 'But,' she added with a laugh as they both looked up at her, 'is all right; is all right; I will make do.'

Catherine folded her lips and said nothing. Martin laughed. 'The lady start to enjoy sheself when she going, yes! Yes, Mammie! Ye-e-s! You not joking!'

Miriam leaned back and smiled at her grandson.

'You're nice, Nan' said Carl, looking at her critically. 'When will you be back?'

'Son, I don't know, non. Is you to come and visit me now!'

'Yes!' said Carl enthusiastically. 'Yes, Nan.' Carl looked from his father to his aunt.

'Don't look at me,' said Catherine. 'That is you and your father business.'

'Dad?'

'Yes. We'll have to plan it. We're overdue for a visit.'

'Well that is all you'll hear now until the date is set.' Catherine drained her orange juice, leaned across and handed a tissue to Carl. 'Wipe your mouth, Carl.'

The three were quiet as they watched Miriam walk through to emigration. She turned and waved, her round face smiling broadly, the light brown hat that she liked to wear perched almost jauntily on her head, her body looking smaller than when she had first arrived, but her face shining with health and happiness. Martin looked down at his sister. Back at his mother. 'Is now I could see how much you two look alike,' he said. 'Short same way. Same round face. And then both of you stubborn same way.'

Catherine chuckled. 'She not joking in truth, you know.'

'Your mother looking well young, you know, girl.'

They waved again. Miriam disappeared around the corner. Carl shouted, 'See you in Grenada, Nan!'

They stood for a while looking at the wall around which Miriam had disappeared. 'Never me again,' said Catherine, as they turned away. 'Never me again.'

'Never me again,' said Miriam to Cousin Milton the next morning. They were sitting under the tamarind tree on the hill just near to her house. 'You see that little devil?' she asked in a lower voice, looking down the hill towards a boy of about six who was moving backwards staring at them, finger in his mouth. 'Is me tambran he coming after, you know. See he see us here, he backing back now. But is me tambran he was coming after.'

Cousin Milton glanced at the retreating youngster, turned his attention back to Miriam. 'But girl, how you mean you don't like England, dey? So England is place not to like, then?

'I don't care what you say!'

'All round you, you seeing England pounds putting up house; all who stay in England for thirty years and more coming back put up house to dead in luxury, you self saying you don't like England? How you mean? Girl, don't talk this thing hard make people laugh at you at all! Keep that to youself!'

Miriam laughed. 'You all right yes, Cousin Milton.

Anyway, that is one episode over! Dead and bury. Not me and England, non. Never me again! Give me a place where I could sit down outside and see people, do what I want. Not me at all. All place have their people! Never me again!'

Milton sighed. Opened his mouth and seemed about to say something. Lapsed into thoughtful silence.

'Never!' pronounced Miriam.

Merle Collins is Grenadian. She lives in London and is a Senior Lecturer in Caribbean Studies at the University of North London. Her published work includes two poetry collections, *Because the Dawn Breaks* (The Women's Press, 1985) and *Rotten Pomerack* (Virago, 1992), a novel, *Angel* (The Women's Press, 1987), and a collection of short stories, *Rain Darling* (The Women's Press, 1990). She is also co-editor of the collection *Watchers and Seekers: Creative Writing by Black Women in Britain* (The Women's Press, 1987).

Red Hibiscus

Joyoti Grech

Red Hibiscus

Serjit said to me, Alone, that's all you ever want to be. Why don't you simply become a hermit for godsakes?

Just because I spent Friday night locked in the flat with Suchitra Mitra turned up to the limits so I couldn't hear the phone ring. I didn't want to talk to anyone asking me to go to Mo's party. Not that I have anything against him, but it was a heavy week and sometimes it's true, solitude is all that I desire, the less I have it the more I want it. Listen, I said to Serjit, if you think I'm a hermit, let me tell you about this girl I used to know.

Remember when Shireen and I had the squat on the Chalk Farm estate? It was halfway through the summer and I'd been working all out on the youth project since the year before and she said if we didn't go away somewhere and get out of this filthy mad city that would be the end of us and I could kiss her goodbye forever. She didn't need to convince me. I wanted a break too. I was just worried about the flat. We'd had the first letter from the council. True it usually takes them a good six months to get their act together after that before you get the eviction order.

Still, you can't be too careful and I did not cherish the thought of leaving the place empty for three weeks. So when someone mentioned – I think it was even you wasn't it Serjit – that their cousin had some friend who'd just got back and didn't have a place to stay, I was ready to hand over the keys and pack my bags right away.

The night before we were due to leave town, the friend came round so we could meet and I could tell her about what day the rubbish is collected and so on. There was a knock at the door and I went to open. There she was with a bag in each hand that pulled her shoulders down into a droop and her hair hanging loose behind. She was wearing a blue cotton shalwar that looked like she'd been born in it and it grew with her as she got older. But clean, and not falling apart either, only, they obviously had a close attachment to each other. We showed her round the place: meters and fusebox; told her to speak to strange men through the letterbox ONLY. We cooked up some food and ate together. Her name was Kamala. Nice person.

Shireen and I got the train next morning and Kamala stayed behind in the flat.

Long afterwards, after I said something one day about friends thinking I was a hermit, she told me about it. And one day after we had talked, she wrote it all out, like a story.

Things went smooth. She took the 21 straight from the end of the street all the way to work on the Charing Cross Road. She worked nights and some matinees on Jeffrey Archer is a Sick Man. She sold ice creams. It didn't take up any brain or soul space.

During the day she would write letters to members of the family she had just left behind for the second time. The first time had been ten years earlier. That had only recently closed over. This visit opened it up again.

Every time she went back, things were a little more different. Some things she couldn't see any more and the ones she could, she didn't always want to.

The first day was Wednesday (we got a Tuesday night train it's cheaper midweek). She wrote to her grandfather, her mother's eldest sister and her second cousin Arati. To Arati she sent all the love she could have put into the word, written down in the language of their own special signs and shared remembered laughter. Thursday to her third uncle's wife's mother, to Laxmipishi and Ghunkumashi. Friday to Babypishi, to her grandfather's cousin's niece, who was at school with her dad and to her uncle Kesup. Saturday was a matinee so she only managed one, long, letter to Arati again and Sunday she was off.

It was the weekend break that did it. Monday she could not go back to work. The thought of that heavy box of Cornettos and Strawberry Sundaes strapped around her neck and the frilly striped apron she had to wear did worse than bring tears to her eyes. It drove her down the road to the Sandhu Stores.

She started with a half a bottle of Gordons and the 2-litre size of tonic water. It was clear and looked like water, which made it seem OK. And ice. Two cubes, clink clink, into the glass, first.

And she asked herself, who shall I write to today? Mona and Leah Nilika, Budhi and Roy and Charudidi. There's never an end to the cousins, always more and always more. And what shall I tell them? About the naked butler and the strawberry lollies and the grey lid that hangs over the city here?

There was no TV in the house, no stereo and the radio batteries ran out by Saturday night. There was a phone, but it wasn't connected. There were pay phones outside the pub but she didn't call anyone.

She got a card from Runa. She pinned it up over the empty fireplace. The picture was a red hibiscus. She couldn't remember if she read what was written on the other side.

The Gordons was still good for a few more shots. When it ran out she checked the tea-caddy and down the sides of the sofa for change and came up with enough at least for a bottle of Thunderbird. Stretched out with lemonade it could get her through the night no problem.

They were very friendly at Sandhu's, for sure. The man behind the counter even gave her a packet of peanuts with the Thunderbird, dropping it into the carrier bag that Kamala held out steady and careful. His brother opened the door for her on the way out and stood there until she made it round the corner into Regent Street. She turned and waved to him.

The front door opened after a series of thumps. Maybe the lock needs to be oiled. She made a note in her head. OIL LOCK. Leaning up against the hallway she kicked the door shut and carried the bags through with both her hands. Thunderbird. Lemonade. Ice. No ice. She made another note. MAKE MORE ICE.

Then one day on her back with the bottles one at the end of

each arm on the dining room floor beside her and her glass carefully balanced on her stomach while she got her breath. With cushions under her head she discovered she could drink lying down. It would be easier with a straw, though. Another note. STRAW.

She sang Rabindrasangeet. Loud and wavy, until her throat was sore, then she cried and fell asleep.

Sunlight in her eyes woke her up around eleven. It was hot through the double glazing and her cheek felt stiff and sticky. In the bathroom mirror her face shone with grease and her nose was red. Her eyes were swollen. She opened her mouth and croaked at the hideous reflection.

Hideous, she said aloud to it.

It was Tuesday and she remembered about the ice creams. Stuff that, she thought.

Later she reasoned it out in terms of the Council might send someone round with the eviction papers and she needed to be in the house, but in the end it was the weight that kept her from going to work. The weight of the ice creams and the weight of the grey lid and the weight of dust and gas in the air that makes it difficult to get up once you lie on your back on the living-room floor.

In the afternoon she dropped by Sandhu's to pick up a few bottles on the way back from the post office. The man called out to his brother in the back and they both looked with great concern at Kamala fishing in her pockets for change.

She felt bad for the brothers seeing her this way so she made up some little story to put their minds at ease about having a few friends round to eat later on. Nothing special you know just a few people. You know how it is. You eat together then you got to have a bit of a drink together. Always the way really.

The brothers didn't look convinced. The older one gave her another pack of peanuts.

Laughing in what she hoped was a carefree manner she picked up her bags and headed back to the house. Days passed,

I think, like this. She fell asleep in the afternoon or early evening, woke at two and four in the morning, and kept always writing long cramped letters on bits of folded blue paper with arrows around the edge.

She dreamt she was at a circus ground with a crowd of other brown-skinned peoples. They were at the dodgem car ride and there were people all around her. She felt that they were safe, because they were together. They were on the Gaza Strip, or the Western Desert in the middle of Australia, or in a reservation in Dakota USA, with a wire fence around the dodgem ride. Or even they were back home in the hills in Bangladesh and the brownskin men were her uncles. One of them told her he was from the Ojibwa nation, but she knew looking in his face it was Gautamkaka.

Other people visited her at odd times of the day and night. She found a note in the hallway from Runa dated Monday.

There's an all-day meeting this Saturday, it said. Where are you? Come round.

Kamala wrote again to Arati.

I dreamt you sent me crates, that I opened up full of red hibiscus. Why don't you write to me? I feel so lonely without you.

Finally a letter came with the postmark on it the shape of her heart and her grandfather's name on the back. He wrote:

Yesterday there was another attack. A man was shot in the market place, the army put out the message that it was our people in the Liberation Force that killed him for informing. The settlers picked up their weapons and many brothers and sisters died fighting in the hours that followed. When the violence broke out the army and police were nowhere in sight. We sent for the Commander. It was four hours before he sent anyone and when they came what they did, they burnt down all our tribal houses and let the settler families go free. When we protested they put troops all around the houses – Chottu will try and give this letter to Babypishi's son, he can take it on the bus to the city when he returns to college tomorrow. Many people including Ghunkumashi's household fled further into the hills, some even made it out of the country but now the army are stopping everyone along the border and holding them in detention camps. Today they are holding all people in the village over 16 in the football stadium because it is the largest enclosed space. Arati cannot write you now, she is in there. You must send this information onwards; be strong and remember that one day we will all be free, not only in the hills but our whole nation, this struggle is not only for us but everyone in the country who is oppressed by the army's guns.

Kamala read it to the end. She thought, people I know are dead. My family is under arrest. Arati cannot write to me because she is in the stadium. I am far away and I am alone. Then she went out to buy another bottle of Thunderbird.

The furniture started to move around, always jumping out to kick her in the shins or bite her on the fleshy part of her thigh as she passed by. The stairs stretched to unclimbable heights. She gave up on the bedroom and bathroom, moved her toothbrush to the kitchen sink.

A brown envelope arrived with a paycheque from the theatre and a note thanking her for her services. Thank you and goodbye. She went out and bought more Thunderbird and a pack of straws.

Runa called again, rapping on the front door and leaning up against the window to try and make out shapes through the thick gauze. Kamala thought she'd gone when she reappeared at the kitchen window, knocking and peering.

Kamala! Runa shouted a few times but Kamala just kept still on the floor. She heard her trample through the long weeds at the side of the house, then the flap of the letterbox as she pushed another note through, and the squeak of her sneakers as she walked away down the road.

I got to try and make some sense of this, Kamala thought, as she checked the winding route of a crack across the ceiling.

Evening came and a siren wailed by down Morden Road. She was dropping off to sleep when her grandmother shook her by the shoulders.

Kamala, she said in the firm voice she used for unpleasant tasks. Get up off your drunken backside.

Kamala woke up. She put all the bottles she could find into a box under the sink. She opened up the windows to let out the dust a little, and plumped up the cushions. Then she brushed her teeth. (She moved her toothbrush back upstairs.) On the way up she found another bottle in the window on the stairway. Her head felt sore and rubbery, her bones ached. She threw up at the taste of the toothpaste. But.

The but was, the day ahead. And in its own time the one after. And the one after that.

Runa's note was still lying in the hallway.

Where are you? Came by to get you to meet this woman Samina Das the woman from Dhaka I told you about. She is here till Friday and has something for you from your COUSIN plus there is a lot she wants to talk about.

Kamala put the note in her pocket. She checked her purse for change and went out to use the phones at the Rising Sun. Red hibiscus flowers bloomed on her mantlepiece.

Joyoti Grech was born in Dhaka, Bangladesh in 1963 when it was still part of Eastern Pakistan. She is the first daughter of a Maltese father and a mother from the indigenous Chakma (Jumma) community of the country's southern hill region. Joyoti was a founding member of the Chittagong Hill Tracts Campaign and Information Network and is a member of the British-based Asian Women's Writers Collective.

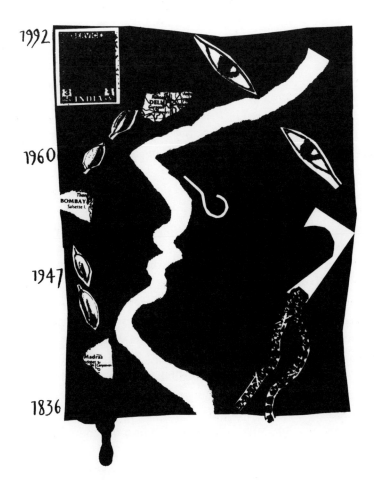

Diary of Home

Maya Chowdhury

Diary of Home

1 January 1992

Last night I dreamt I was packing my clothes, frantically gathering my things at midnight. Every time I asked my father a question he answered in Urdu. I tried to make sense of it. He kept telling me 'Urdu bol, Urdu bol . . . speak in Urdu, don't ask why.' 'I'll pack in the morning. Why now? Why now?' We left most of our things behind.

Today was winter, there was no sun and I knew I was in Britain. I read my book *A History of India 2*. I never read part one; I was in too much of a hurry to find out. I wanted to find the answers to a dream.

I sit in the kitchen, at the table, burning a candle; my shadows dance on the ceiling. I look at jars of lentils and spices in the dim light. They haunt me, tease me, pass judgement. There is nothing written down. It's passed by voice; stories in the night, stories that keep us growing. The voices have died; I have no stories to keep.

I went down to Crammond, walking along the beach and watched the waves fill and empty rock pools. I walked along seaweed-covered rocks, slipping from side to side, my eyes peering at the cold estuary disappearing into the grey of the sky.

I thought about the sea travelling. She knows no cease-fire line or the difference between a European and an Indian body, except the sea knows me. My brown skin travels from the Rann of Kutch to the Firth of Forth, unravelling around the coasts of the world. Travelling from the Arabian Sea to the North Sea, the sea travels across oceans and does not know that one country has ended and another begun, that the spices in Sainsbury's travel, that the silk in Liberty's travels, that people travel. Except the sea finds their bodies on her ocean bed and unpicks their flesh until they are bones, and only the sea knows where she has hidden them.

Our house was at one end of the village, a small stone
house, with a courtyard and some trees. There was a kitchen, a
main room, two bedrooms and an outside bathroom. One
bedroom was my parents' and the other was ours; the boys and
girls were divided by a hanging cloth.

We always lived with the sun; daylight brought the sun and
night the stars. I sat in the courtyard in my pyjamas drinking
hot milky tea, counting the stars. I always awoke in my bed in
the morning, hot and sticky, my sheet twisted around my feet.

1 February 1992

Tomorrow is my birthday. I will be 28. Twenty-eight years in
the present, but what of the past? I get out an airmail letter.

Dear Auntie,

Remember the story you told me about my dad, uncles and
aunts crossing the border? You never did tell me the name of
the place they came from, or the day. I have been in the
library all week looking for dates and places . . . What was
the tribe? What was the original name?

So how is everyone? How is Delhi? It must be getting warm
there. It seems so long ago that I was there. I wish I could
come and visit; maybe this year.

Tell me how everyone is. Write soon.

I go straight to the post-box. The wind is icy. I forget to put my
gloves on. I walk back wondering what to do for my birthday.
I'm getting too old for birthday cakes; it would be an inferno
with all those candles on; keep my hands warm anyway.

It's five years today since I left for India. I remember I went
just after my birthday. I wanted to be one year older before I
left.

*I overhear my parents saying it was going to be a long walk,
'Too long for the children,' my mother said. 'Well what can we
do? We can't leave them behind; we have to go.' I hide behind
a tree, trying to be quiet so they wouldn't know I was snooping. There was a mosquito buzzing in my ear. I try to swot it
with a twig; it makes a loud crack. I run and run until I am at
the end of the field and I hide behind some bushes, breathless.
When I catch my breath I walk back calmly as if I'd been
playing down the end of the field. My father is nowhere to be
seen and my mother is chopping onions. I want to tell my
brother and sisters but I am too scared. I try to imagine where
we'd be walking to and think of my dreams.*

1 March 1992

I've been waiting a month and still no news; maybe I'm the
only one who wants to remember the past.

*Suddenly in the night we are gathering our things; we leave
our home within a few minutes. I pick up a book, one or two
clothes and that is it. I wrap my things in a cloth and hold it
over my shoulder. We begin walking, no one speaks, no one
asks why, or where we are going. I try to count the stars as we
walk. It is hot and I am tired; I want to be in my bed asleep.*

Today I phone my mum, searching for memories. I stand in
the hallway, twisting the telephone coil first one way then the
other.

'Yes I remember. Your grandfather didn't think the partition would happen; he lost all his money, didn't withdraw it
when everyone else did. He was an optimist, your grandfather.
I think doctors have to be. He was stubborn too, like your dad.
He wouldn't listen to your grandmother. She said it would
happen. Your dad said she kept reading your grandfather bits
out of the newspaper; he just shrugged his shoulders, and went
to work mumbling that the newspaper was just propaganda
and lies. He didn't want it to happen. I think your dad took
after your grandfather.'

'What else?'

'Nothing; that's all I know. Why don't you write to your auntie?'

'I have; no reply.'

'Hmm, maybe everyone has forgotten.'

I put down the phone and make some tea. Indian tea, milky with cardamom pods. Should I write to my aunt again? I sit drinking tea, thinking about my grandfather and my father. I wonder when my father had told my mother the story. She couldn't remember, and my father's been dead nine years now and the dead can't speak.

1 April 1992

April fool's day. I make dahl and rice and fool myself I'm happy here. I'm so busy searching for memories I burn the dahl. It sticks to the bottom of the pan, scorched and lumpy. I eat it anyway, putting on loads of chilli sauce to take away the burnt taste.

I remember when I was a student and my flatmate was studying history. I read her essay about British atrocities in India during the Raj. The memory burns me, scars my life here. I look at skinheads on the street with knives and I see my dead ancestors licking the blood spilt of their family from the steps of their houses. Anger freezes me, pulls me towards the kitchen drawer. I finger the blade of the bread knife; scalloped steel tortures my memories. I toast the bread and read chapter three – A History of India 2. India is a concept, invented by the British for trade purposes, for conquering purposes, for blood purposes, for power.

The sun sets over the castle; the sky is red and blue. I climb out the attic window and sit on the roof thinking of home, wondering where home is. Last week I went to London again. I got off the 15:19 train and nearly got on the 15.20 back to Edinburgh. Travelling scares me; I forget where I'm going.

My feet keep sticking in the mud. I have one chappal on

and one is lost. I throw the other away. I am nearly running to keep up. My mother is striding ahead and I don't know where my father is. We stop to play once or twice but Mother shouts at us to keep walking. She speaks in Urdu too.

We see our burnt-out houses on the way. What is going on? 'Was it in the newspaper?' I ask my mother. 'Shshh,' my brother says, 'keep walking, not talking.'

I went to India five years ago. Yesterday I got out my notebook and photographs. I drew a map of my journeys from Delhi to Madras, Bombay to Kashmir and back again. I crumpled up the paper and threw it out of the window of my tenement flat. I watched it fall heavily and crash on the pavement below. I was looking in the wrong place. I should have gone to Pakistan.

I was at home pulling water from a well, shelling tamarind pods, standing on a cliff edge on a hill station in Rajasthan looking out at the desert, dry hot wind in my hair and eyes. I was at home lighting candles for Diwaali, buying mangoes in the market in the hot sticky dark of 7.30. I was at home sitting on the doorstep for four hours, head covered in Mendhi.

My aunt hasn't written back. Seems like she wants to forget her relatives in England, or maybe I'm being hard on her. She loved me like her own daughter when I was there. Maybe I should go back, start again. After all, I was looking in the wrong place last time.

1 May 1992

I get up early and walk around the park looking for signs of summer. The dew is quietly evaporating as the sun peeks out from behind the clouds. The grass smells fresh, smells like summer might come soon.

I think my aunt didn't get the letter, but I'm too scared to write to find out in case she doesn't want to communicate. Mum says write again, there's no harm, no shame; there's nothing to be ashamed about living in England. It didn't feel like than when I went; they said I ate roti like an Indian. I never knew what they meant exactly. I tried to ignore it and eat my dinner.

Well I certainly can't cook like a nice Indian bride, unless of course you like thick rubbery dahl and overdone rice. While I'm here being vegetarian because it makes sense, they're all there eating meat because it makes sense to them and shows they are well off. When I went there, it didn't make sense.

I sit down and watch *EastEnders*, trying not to think too hard about sense.

I don't know why we are dressed like Moslems, why we have to speak in Urdu, why it is so muddy and dangerous. I just know the newspapers had a lot to say and I don't really know what that was about either. I'm ten, I can read but I don't always know what things mean, or what some words are. I haven't got a dictionary to look up words; it got left behind, and anyway there aren't any newspapers to read now.

My bundle is heavy. I am so tired and weak, my mother says leave it behind but I want the book so I leave the clothes behind a tree, tie the book up in the cloth and start walking again.

When *EastEnders* finishes I put the TV off. There was once an Indian family in it; not any more though. Seems like the novelty has worn off. It's AIDS these days, though it's important too. Millions of people watch *EastEnders* and see no Asian people; millions of people don't have to know we exist. In the unrepresentative TV stakes we are 9 am Sunday, Channel 4.

1 June 1992

Now the sun will shine all month, makes my hair look more shiny, or maybe it's the Mendhi I put in it once a month. Did I do it last month?

We walk for days. 'Why can't we get the bus?' I keep asking. 'It's too dangerous,' comes the ridiculous reply. I shut

up and keep walking. What if it is really too dangerous? I'm
scared and cling onto the end of my mother's sari. We are
splashed in mud from head to toe, our white pyjamas speckled
like a rooster's feathers. My mother has big lumps of mud
hanging from the end of her green cotton sari.

'Why are we leaving? Because our Gods aren't safe here,
because we're not safe here. But I thought Gods were supposed
to look after us, how can they not be safe? Because of human
beings, because humans are stupid. Well, if they're so stupid,
why are we running away from them? Because they're stupid
and dangerous.'

I try out a new dahl recipe and ask a friend round for
dinner. We have Vienetta for dessert and talk politics all night.
I wonder why I even consider politics. I realise it considers me;
my skin is political and I can't ignore its questions.

I sit in the kitchen after she's gone. The candle has burnt
down halfway. I look around at the jars of lentils and spices
and wonder if this is my home.

1 July 1992

Mogul emperors haunt me. I find a building in Edinburgh with
a sign saying East India Company. I feel sick. I feel so related
to this city and to India, I am torn apart and my flesh is ripped.
The ribbons make a flag for Edinburgh Castle, banners in
India.

I walk down the street. I feel as if someone's watching me,
as if it's 1947 and I have to escape death. In 1947, ten and a
half million people changed sides, quarter of a million lost their
lives. I dash out in front of a speeding taxi. It narrowly misses
me. Changed sides; what does that mean?

I don't understand religion; if it's so sacred why is there so
much death? If it's above life, then why do we exist anyway? I
sit in a cafe in the Grassmarket and look at old photographs of
Edinburgh. What did it look like in 1947?

We have been walking for days now, but I begin to under-

stand why there are dead people at the side of the road and in the wheat fields, why it is muddy. I want to run. If it is so dangerous here, why can't we get there, to the other side? Why is it taking so long? We stop and eat some hard, dry roti and I don't want to sit. I keep looking around thinking we might die at any moment.

I look at my mother, my brothers and sisters. Why do they not panic and run and run until we get to the other side? I realise we are too weak and tired to run.

My parents came to Edinburgh in 1960. They found it hard to find a flat to rent. My dad was a doctor, a good occupation. His skin was the wrong colour though. In 1981 I too looked for a flat in Edinburgh. I was a student but my skin was still the wrong colour. It's 1992 now I'm not looking for a flat; I'm looking for home.

1 August 1992

It's hot for Edinburgh, like the nearest to monsoon weather we'll ever get here. Everyone has their shorts on as if it's the Fourth of July. I never wore shorts in India; it was too hot and made you too naked for the culture. I sit in the park feeling naked, as if my culture is showing through and everyone can see it. I take off my Indian sparkly earrings and put them in my pocket.

We weave in and out of the countryside, crossing fields, passing small villages, houses. Sometimes we hear voices shouting in the distance. We cross a main junction and there's blood all over the road. My mother looks worried. We all hold hands and run and run as much as we can until we collapse behind some bushes. I want to ask my mother about the blood but I'm scared of the answer. I look down at my Moslem clothes. We might die either way. Moslems might pull down our pyjamas and see that we were not circumcised, and Hindus or Sikhs might think we're Moslems in these clothes. I want to walk naked, then I'll be allowed to live.

It's getting dark, the park is dim and shadowy. I realise I've been sitting for hours; it's getting cold and I shiver. I walk down the street wandering in and out of the shops. I buy some rice and Bolst curry powder at the corner shop – Eight 'til Late.

'I've seen you before,' the Indian woman at the till smiles. I smile back. 'Where you from then?'

'Here, I was born here.'

'In Edinburgh?' she sounds surprised. 'Yes, but you know, where are you from?'

'My dad was Indian, from the Punjab.'

'Oh. I'm Punjabi too. Can you speak it?'

'No, well you see everyone ended up in Delhi, so they spoke Hindi mainly.'

'Oh, not Sikh then?'

'No. Well my grandmother was.'

'Oh!' She gives me a puzzled look.

But then, when my grandparents were young, it wasn't such a big deal a Hindu and a Sikh marrying. I know it wasn't just that she was puzzled about, but I hadn't got a spare day to begin to explain the history.

1 September 1992

I found a book of my dad's today. *Gray's Anatomy*; it was very vivid and colourful. That's why I couldn't look at it; can't stand the sight of blood and flesh. It was such an old copy it's probably a collectors' item. I put it back on the shelf and thought about Pakistan.

My brother says we've walked forty miles. I feel like we've been walking for a year. Maybe we managed five miles a day, walking with tired souls, with only the moon to light our journey through sugar cane and over wheat fields.

I get out some old maps of India, trace the Mogul Empire in 1605, from Kabul to Bengal. My finger weaves in and out of the provinces. I turn to 1836. India was a patchwork of territories striped with colonial boundaries. The whole world had to go to war twice to change this map. The map was changed by a line which looked for the religion of the population, which followed rivers not reason.

I put the maps away and think about the lines of Hindus and Moslems crossing this line.

1 October 1992

I examine my bank balance. This is the best month to travel to India, *post* hot season, *post* monsoon climate. Just right for someone brought up on snow and North Sea winds. No good; it's in the red. Maybe next year.

We walk and I try to forget the faces of the rotting bodies I've seen. I try to forget how much blood. I decide I will be a doctor like my father. I decide I will save lives.

I November 1992

I forget when Diwaali is. It was November 5th last year so I celebrate it on the first of November, burning candles and sending some 'Happy New Year' cards. I'm confused. I'm supposed to send them in January and I don't really know what or why I'm celebrating. My Moslem friend goes for all the festivals, Christmas, Easter, Eid, Diwaali, any excuse for a rave up, she says. I agree and put up the Xmas tinsel around the mirror in the bathroom.

We meet our father in a small village. It is dark; I can only just make out his face. We hug and cry. I never thought I would see him again. He cries and holds my mother. He has some roti and we eat, quietly sobbing.

He gives us each a burqa and we walk off into the night dressed as Moslem women. Five more miles and then we must throw off our disguises if we want to stay alive. Five more miles to the end of our journey across the Punjab, province of five rivers, now a river of blood.

1 December 1992

Xmas parties and lots of tinsel. Mine is still hanging in the
bathroom from last month. Maybe I'll just leave it up all year
round, for all the different festivals. I'm looking in the mirror,
putting on my sparkly earrings to go out. I found them in the
pocket of my summer jacket when I was trying it on. Funny
how you wear your thinnest clothes in winter and your thickest
in summer, when it rains all the time.

*It rains and the pain of the camp flows out like dirty
monsoon water. We are sent to Chandigarh and my father
stays in the refugee camp mending slaughtered bodies, trying to
contain the illness and despair which spreads like cholera.*

*We travel by train from Amritsar; the wooden floors of the
train are stained red. I know this is just the beginning of my
journey.*

My aunt gave me them, the earrings, when I was in India. I
never did hear from her. I know she didn't get my letter. I
should write again but I think I know the answer myself.

I dream about a journey, but it's not mine; it's hot and
muddy and dangerous. Maybe it's a premonition.

Maya Chowdhury was born in Edinburgh. At present based in
Sheffield, she is a member of the Asian Women's Writers Collective
and works as a writer, film-maker and photographer. She has written
for film and radio and her work (poetry, short stories, plays) has been
published in various anthologies and magazines. She is co-author of a
poetry collection entitled *Putting in the Pickle where the Jam Should
Be.* She has won several accolades for her work: in 1991, winner of
the BBC Radio Young Playwrights' Festival, in 1992, the Cardiff
International Poetry Competition, and in 1993, the Littlewoods Arc
Short Story competition and runner-up in the Poetry Business Competition.

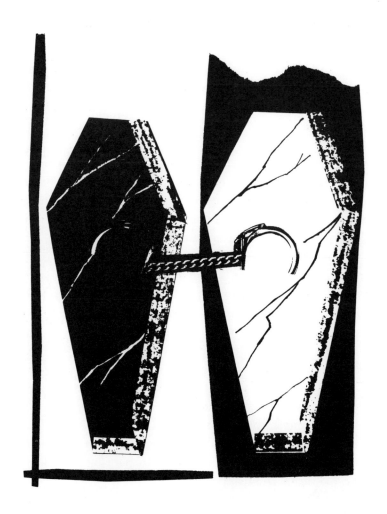

The Dead Men Who Lost Their Bones

Mandla Langa

The Dead Men Who Lost Their Bones

They call me Clementine, here, although that is not my real name; but since I don't own a single thing here – the drab grey tunics and dresses I put on and, come to that, even myself – it does not matter anymore. A lot of things have ceased to matter.

My twin sister, Benedicta (and that is not her real name, either) is here with me. This is a home that is a cross between a reform school and an orphanage. There are some pretty tough kids here: and the sisters are quick to punish for infringements like wetting the bed or using bad language.

Benedicta and I are twelve years old this year, and it is close to Christmas. The place is pleasant, though, despite the unexpected punishments. Everyone, the Sisters, that is, seems to be fighting a war to make us forget what happened in the past, the events that brought us here.

Many other children here have many terrible tales to tell. We eat a lot, more, in fact, than back home, but Benedicta and I are increasingly – daily – getting thinner and thinner. I guess food can never be a substitute for what the spirit hankers for. It is all very simple: we miss our parents.

I can't understand why this knowledge escapes the Sisters and the Matron especially, since they are holy and knowledgeable and highly cultured people.

It was Papa who went first; Mama didn't die in the way that people die and are made one with the groaning earth. When she lost her baby – I understood this much, much later – to the shock of Papa's death, all light left her eyes: she would stare and stare and stare at the walls of our homestead. The social workers came and took her to a place for people who can no longer be responsible for their actions. Her mind had taken the long, returnless journey into the very jaws of oblivion.

It was the social workers' idea to bring us here.

Someone said that we sanctify and immortalise things by giving them words or names. There are words, now, I am forced to utter – usually in the loneliness of my bed, in the snarling silence of the midnight hour. Words like, *Mama, Papa, Our House.*

Our house, in reality, belonged to Meneer Gert Visser. He was a farmer and my father – in fact, all of us, at one time or the other – worked for him. It was a beautiful farm. Mevrou Visser was a kindly woman with hair the colour of ripe orange-rinds and eyes as blue and opaque as cut glass. She experimented with all kinds of plants, this remarkable woman, surprising us by dirtying her hands, digging the black earth, planting such things as flowers: zinnias and chrysanthemums; and exotic and unheard of foods like okra and plantains.

There were always bees hovering around the flowers, hovering angrily around her, so that bees and Mevrou Visser somehow get confused in my mind.

We had the job, my sister and I, to water the growing things, keeping away from the bees, early in the morning before undertaking the long trek to school, and late in the afternoon after the sun had made its silent but reluctant farewell.

Mother's chores revolved mainly around making sure that her family – and the Visser family – were kept well fed. She also cleaned up their house.

It was a big house, painted white; the whole homestead was surrounded by a high, barbed-wire fence. This, I was told, was to keep dangerous animals from sneaking in in the evenings and killing calves, lambs and kids.

Sometimes Baas Visser, as he was known, came into the farm with a squad of black men in chains. They would be given sacks to wear and would toil the whole day under the broiling sun in the fields that certainly looked endless, planting or reaping. These were bad men, I was told, and deserved to be sjambokked – as usually happened to one or two particularly hardened cases – and had a white prison guard riding a horse between the mielie rows supervising them.

The guard never forgot his rifle and his sjambok. I never forgot the eyes of the condemned men. At sundown they were chained – the way my father chained a span of oxen – and huddled together in a barn.

Mama didn't like her job; she hated the farm. She was heavy with child, so I guess she tired very easily. She carped a lot because Papa never seemed to do anything all day long except act as gun carrier for Baas Visser when they went hunting.

My father was perhaps the most handsome man I have ever seen. Whether he was in tattered overalls or his Sunday best, he managed – God knows how, because I know how harried he must have been – to look as unruffled as ever. He had that detached air of someone perpetually preoccupied, someone wrestling with something deep and unutterably strangling. He must have loved Mama very much.

That one evening, for instance, Papa was on the verandah, cleaning his master's guns. To me, they looked like the rifle that was so much part of the guard who strutted arrogantly, on horseback.

In our little dining-room, the table was set.

'Go call your father,' Mama said. 'There's some warm water in the basin for him to wash his hands.'

I rushed outside. 'Papa?' I called. He looked up at me; there was a pale moon shining that evening, drenching the deserted farm, investing it with a cold pallor. The moonlight caught my father's face, filling his eyes with dancing things.

'Yes, Tee?' Papa always called me Tee.

'Mama says to come in. Food is ready.' I watched his hands as he cradled the barrels of the guns; his hands were shiny with oil. He picked up some waste cloth and wiped his hands. He went to the basin and soaped his hands. Cleansed after this ablution that was almost a ritual, he went into the house.

Already seated at the table, Mama said, 'Love, I've always said I don't want you cleaning those awful guns around the house.' She was not really angry. She was tired.

'Aw, ma,' Papa said, sitting down beside Benedicta, 'where do you expect me to clean them – in the barn?' He shovelled a spoonful of gravy-soaked pap into his mouth. He chewed absent-mindedly.

'I don't care where you do it,' Mama said, not to be out-done. 'I don't care. You could clean those guns sitting in Mevrou's flower-bed for all I care.'

'Now, wouldn't that be something?' Papa said, smiling. Then he turned to Benedicta. 'And how was my little girl's school-day today?'

'It was all right, Papa,' Benedicta said. 'We've got a new teacher from the Boland. She was introduced during the assembly time.' There was something bubbling in Benedicta's voice, an anticipation. 'And when asked to say something, she told us to pray for this troubled country – and for the Prime Minister.'

Papa laughed, but it was the choked, mirthless laughter that was hollow and infinitely mocking. 'Well,' he said, 'if you ask me, the white people here had better pray for *their* country. As for *their* Prime Minister, he'll soon know better than to run a country as though it were a taxi service.'

Mama's face was grave, indecipherable. 'Let's just please eat,' she commanded. We ate in silence for some time. Papa let his spoon drop on his plate, the sound surprisingly loud and jarring.

'You know,' Papa said, 'I figure someday very soon we're going to have to leave this farm. I'm up to here with the way things are happening around here.' There was a grating tone in Papa's voice; it had thickened considerably.

'What has happened now?' Mama asked, laying her spoon on the plate before her. Was there something like fear in her voice? '*Kwenzenjani manje, baba wabantwana bami* – what has happened now, father of my children?' She poured some coffee into thick mugs.

'You know,' Papa said, 'since Baas Visser got that stupid Skotnes boy to take care of the culling and dipping of cattle, nothing has ever gone right. That boy carries on like a regular slave-driver. I have never liked him, anyway, with a face like the underbelly of a crocodile. He calls those men from prison *kaffirs*. Kaffir this, kaffir that!' He looked at his coffee-mug as though the dark, swirling beverage held the key to a deep and impenetrable secret.

'Today we drove to the hardware store to get a ploughshare sharpened. On the way we saw a big snake crossing the road, leisurely. It must have been a rinkhals, and you know how dangerous that type is. I thought that the Skotnes boy would wait until the snake had slithered into the grass, or even swerve and avoid it. You think he'd do the sensible thing? But no. He swerved to run over the snake. I don't know whether he succeeded in hitting the snake or not, but that doesn't matter, you just don't do a damnfool thing like that with a rinkhals, or with *any* snake, for that matter. You just don't fool around with a snake, doesn't this boy have some sense!

'And, then, you know what happened?' We all knew that Papa was not waiting for an answer. He took out his pipe from the bib of the overalls and filled it; he used a piece of paper to burn the tobacco from the candle flame. There was a stertorous sound as he sucked at his pipe until the tobacco was burning evenly.

'Just when that no-good fool tried to hit the snake,' Papa went on, 'the van conked out. Kaput. And –' here Papa's voice thickened with rage, '–he said I must go out and push. I said, "What?" He said, "Get out and push the blerry van." I looked at him in disbelief. "You mean I must get out and push the van after you've tried to hit a snake, do you think I'm *crazy*?" He said, "Boy, get out and push the blerry van," and I said, "You're out of your blerry mind," and he got so angry – his face so red – that he balled his fists and I could see that he was ready to strike me. And I said, "White boy, just try that once and you'll see the eyes of a worm, I'm not the one who bought you this scrap." I think he saw it in my eyes that I would kill him there and then. After much tinkering with the ignition and the accelerator, the car jumped forward. We got to the hardware store and left the ploughshare there. When he dropped me here, on our return, he said he'd certainly report me to Baas Visser. I told him to report me to the *Volksblad*, it wouldn't turn a hair on my head.'

Even at that age, I knew a certain code – unspoken and unwritten – between a master and a servant who had served him for a long time. I knew that Papa had nothing to fear from the Skotnes boy; Baas Visser, if he were to be told of Papa's insubordination, would simply ooh-aah, but nothing would come of it. The master and servant are connected by an umbilical cord that would put both men on the gates of Hell were it to be severed.

That night we helped Mama with the dishes; Mama made the usual evening prayer. Whether by omission or design, we did not pray for the Prime Minister and the sons and daughters of the masters of the land.

The story gets increasingly hard to tell here.

I remember that Benedicta and I came back from school and found Mama looking grave and troubled. I felt that there was something terribly wrong. I don't know how I felt this, but then this is one of the things that gets terribly hard to explain. I felt menace hanging over the air like a pall; the first thought that came to me was, *Where's Papa?* My trepidation was heightened by the presence of other people – some I'd never seen before – from the other houses on the farm. What was even more frightening was the fact that people – these strangers, were comforting Mama, saying words like, 'Don't fret, now, everything will be all right.'

For a moment we all thought that everything would be all right when Papa burst into the house, his normally ragged overalls looking as though he had been locked in a life-and-death struggle with a particularly ravenous man-eating beast. His eyes – my father's eyes – held the same expression I'd seen on the condemned faces of the manacled men in sacks.

Before Papa could say anything, in that confused babel of

voices, I rushed to him and clasped him around the knees in a grip I had a feeling that even death could not undo. Slowly, wearily, my father sat down and I sat on his lap. Benedicta, her hands on his chair, looked up at the people in the room, her eyes as eloquent as the ages.

'What happened?' This was asked by someone I didn't see; it could have been Mama. But, then, my mother – who certainly knew that our normally unflappable father was at that very moment being menaced by something more consuming, more unspeakable and more ravaging than the most roaring inferno – could not have asked anything. She was beyond questioning.

Before Papa could answer, there was the barking of dogs. Boots crunched on the gravel outside, and three policemen entered without knocking. The silence that followed their entry was more deafening than the wailing of a thousand alley cats. Two policemen were white; the third one, an African, looked like Thembi's father. Thembi sat next to me in class.

'*Wie's Simon Ngozi?*' This was asked by one of the white policemen. I looked at him, his peaked cap, the carefully creased and laundered serge uniform, the shining holster and the brown boots. I looked at the faces of the white policemen – their cold, blue eyes and thin bloodless lips – as they looked at all of us, their eyes boring into ours as though trying to break an ancient, indecipherable coded message.

My father stood up. He didn't say anything.

'*Jy's Simon Ngozi?*' another disembodied voice asked. Papa nodded.

The black policeman took out a pair of handcuffs. The silver handcuffs looked strange in the black hands of the black man; the jagged edges danced cruelly in the dim light of the candle; it was as though the edges were live things, with a life of their own.

'*Wag so 'n bietjie, Ngobese* – wait a minute,' one of the policemen admonished, laying a restraining, pinkish-brown hand on Ngobese's eager wrist. Ngobese, thoroughly chastised, cringed. '*Ek soek die man moet ons se wat het regtig angegaan* – I want this man to tell us what really happened.' There was something menacingly conciliatory about this policeman's demeanour. This, somehow, was more sinister than if the man had acted outright hostile.

'I left this morning,' Papa began, his voice cracking, weary, weary, 'with Baas Visser to our usual hunting spot in the mountain. It is very rocky, this hunting spot, and full of treacherous precipices. "We have to be careful, Baas," I told the Baas; but, then –' there was something immeasurably sad and wry that flickered across Papa's face – 'but, then, he told me he had been hunting on these grounds since he was this high.'

Papa was silent. He swallowed something that must have tasted like the bitterest herb. 'And then we saw a springbok darting out of a thicket into a clearing in the woods. I gave him his .303, and he told me that the springbok would be heading our way. It seems like something startled it, for it soon bolted right back into the woods, some distance away.

'Baas Visser motioned for me to be as stealthy as possible and try to approach our quarry from the other end, out of the wind. He went straight for it, keeping to the left. I got round the thicket and he went his way. I could not see him, then, the place is dense. After a moment, I heard the loud crack of a rifle, then there was silence, then there was a scream.'

There was a loud wailing outside and a thoroughly distraught, dishevelled Mevrou Visser came into the house, screaming, '*Waar's my man? Waar's my man?*' and the two white policemen – who were certainly the only reassuring faces Mevrou Visser saw – held her, with great tenderness. The black policeman, who would have no role in the consoling of this pathetic white woman, looked as though he was beginning to doubt the wisdom of his presence in the house.

The white policemen murmured words to Mevrou Visser. We all looked at the scenario being enacted before us: all frozen in some dreadful moment in time, the scared eyes of the neighbours, Mama who looked stunned, the silently sobbing

Mevrou Visser: and I had a feeling that this was just another nightmare. We would all wake up tomorrow and talk about it; everything was going to be all right.

It became a nightmare. The policeman handcuffed my father, his face a mask of triumphant mockery, and steered him out of the house into the waiting Land Rover. (This is not really an arrest; we just want him to show us the spot, all right?) All right. Mama stood supporting herself on the table. Just when I was about to rush to Papa outside, I saw with the aid of the turning Land Rover's headlamps that streams of something dark were coursing down my mother's legs, down to her bare feet, becoming drops that turned into a dark puddle.

'Mama,' I screamed, 'you're bleeding!'

Mama lost the baby that night; Papa lost his life. The police came back around midnight and talked to an old woman who was watching over us because, you see, whilst Papa and the police were on their way to the mountain, Mama was on her way to the hospital (some eighteen miles away) in an ox-wagon.

They – the police – said that when they went to do an inspection in loco – whatever that means! – my father slipped and plummeted down, down the precipice.

The police were convinced that the spot where my father perished was almost certainly the same spot where Baas Visser had begun his fateful journey into eternity. It was a crying shame, the police said, but such things have been known to happen, and the bodies have not been found, it's dark – so we'll see what tomorrow brings.

Tomorrow brought two coffins – a groaning weight – supported by an ox-wagon my father had helped make. There was silence that day; the wind did not blow, crickets and frogs were rendered mute, dogs put their tails between their legs, skulked away and forgot to bark at strangers.

Separate funeral services were held. Both coffins had been sealed, the police informed us, because the bodies had been too terribly mutilated in the dreadful plunges.

When Mama returned from the hospital, her womb ruined, she was no longer fit, the social workers said, to stay with us. They took her screaming, to the mental asylum called Fort Napier, in Pietermaritzburg. When they took her away, she did not look like our mother any more. They promised, the people who brought us here, that they would bring her back to us, as fit as a fiddle.

They are lying, of course. They never brought her back, they took us away instead. I am still wondering to this day, though, whether the still and broken body in the casket we had interred into the yawning, still and broken ground, really belonged to my father.

We will wait.

Mandla Langa was born in South Africa. He is the author of two novels, *Tenderness of Blood* (Zimbabwe Publishing House, 1987) and *A Rainbow in the Paper Sky* (Kliptown Books, London, 1989). In 1991 he won a Writers' Bursary from the Arts Council and has recently completed his third novel, *The Cult of Innocence*, to be published later this year. He has also contributed to various poetry and short story collections and is presently co-writing a screenplay for a film on South Africa.

The Canebreakers

Jacob Ross

The Canebreakers

. . . no-no-no! No regrets. You see, it was something more than just an idea, really. Was, erm, a kind of responsibility if you like: a legacy. Something my sister pointed me towards and kept on pointing at, over the years, till I suddenly stopped staring at her finger and really looked to see where she was pointing.

In fact, I've been thinking that it will be your turn soon. We need doctors now; builders, menders – makers of new roads. And always, I think, people like my sister to keep pointing out the way. Y'all unnerstan – no? Never mind. It will make sense as I go along. Just sit up and listen.

I used to watch the women coming home from work, wading ever so heavily, ever so tiredly, through the thick, orange light, their frocks fluttering like wide, grey wings. I would stand on the only, giant boulder in our yard and from there, peer down and over the fields of sugar cane searching among that crawling line for my sister.

I strived to pick her out, not by her face – dusk and distance wouldn't allow it – but by that long stride of hers and the curious way her body angled forward when she walked; as though pushing against winds felt only by herself. But they were no more than evening shapes, dark against the white feeder road that stretched way behind and beyond them till the distance narrowed it to a needlepoint.

'Sis,' I asked once, when she reached home, 'why I could never mek you out from mongst all dem odder wimmen, comin home from work?'

I remember asking with great solemnity, affected as usual, by the air of seriousness that she perpetually carried with her, almost like another garment.

'Coz wee'z de same, ah s'pose,' she answered, pausing to consider, then repeating: 'yep, wee'z de same. Sides, y'all men never choose de right light to look for us in.'

I didn't know what she meant by that. In fact, I didn't know what she meant by most of the answers she gave to my questions. The truth is, my sister hardly ever talked straight. Most people thought she never talked at all. For me, whenever she did, it was to say things that confused me greatly.

I used to think it was the canes that had her like that. I mean, any person would feel small and confused and lost in those puny, spider-legged houses of ours, standing like so many ugly, four-sided crafts at the very edges of a wild, green, tossing ocean of sugar canes.

Dry season, the time of reaping, she became more firm-lipped and even more silent than before. It was not like a sudden change of mood. Rather, it was something that happened slowly, a sort of deepening inside that grew with the growing of the canes, with their foam-like blossoming and, finally, their ripening in dry season.

I sometimes looked at Sis and found myself wondering about my mother. I couldn't recall what she looked like; though people said my sister was her spitting image. I must have missed her because I sometimes dreamt of this woman, of indistinguishable features, who had returned from Trinidad and taken me back there with her to meet a stepfather, a brother and a little sister I had only heard about.

It was rumoured that Sis had been given the chance to live with my mother and she had not taken it. It was the year after Ma had left us. I was four, my sister, eighteen.

The boat ticket had arrived from Trinidad and my sister's departure date was confirmed. Farewell kisses and speeches were thrown at her like confetti. She had taken it all in, impassively, and had left the following morning dressed for Trinidad, clutching the brown cardboard suitcase in her right hand.

Imagine the confusion when, about half an hour or so later, the workers on the estate saw her come in the taxi she had left with, borrow a machete and set to work, still dressed in her best dress – as if leaving for Trinidad and returning twenty minutes later were the most natural things in the world. She had said one of those puzzling things that I had, by now, grown accustomed to hearing from her.

'You have ter *break* cane, not *escape* cane. Somebody have to stay. Sides, it have cane in Trinidad too.'

She had taken me back – from my aunt's – to live with her in the house my mother had fled.

Sis got up very early every morning, waking me also. It would be so still, you could hear the canes rubbing leaves and get the smell of burnt sugar and rum from the big factory miles away. She told me where to tie the goats for the day. And while I was out, she prepared the day's lunch – mainly boiled vegetables, salt fish and a hot drink of black sage leaves or lemon grass which also served as breakfast.

She then tied her head and wrapped a strong band of cloth around her waist. Barefoot and straight-backed, she would stride out into the morning, the little machete held easily in one hand, the old, fire-blackened tin marked DANO MILK which contained her lunch, cupped carefully in the other.

She never said goodbye. But I didn't mind, because she was that way and I had grown accustomed to her silence.

Later, I would leave for school, balancing my books with the same care that Sis had held her cutlass; my lunch, in an identical can, carried in the other hand.

I never discussed school with Sis. She never asked. I simply told her what I wanted and she got it. I would hand her the slip of paper, folded exactly as the teacher had given it, with the name of the book he had scribbled there. Sis would take it delicately between her fingers, as though afraid of hurting it and, without glancing, place the note where she kept the little things she valued – her money mostly – in the cleft of her bosom.

One night I woke up and caught her staring at the slip I had brought from school with *The Student's Companion* written in my teacher's bold handwriting. She did not know I was awake and studying her face in the lamplight. I will never forget that picture of her, sitting on the edge of the little bed, squinting at the paper, her lips forming, ever so slowly, ever so painfully, letters, words – a wish? It must have been half an hour before she sighed, folded the slip carefully and placed it on the bedside table.

That very Saturday, she got up early, put on what I had come to call her 'Trinidad dress' and left for St George's on foot.

She returned in the afternoon with the new book and, like all the times before, asked me to open it while she sat in the corner, near the window, staring at me with such a strange expression, I felt nervous and proud and foolish at the same time.

I used to take these things for granted – I mean, getting up on mornings, tethering the goats, watching the people leave their homes and head like a great, long column of worker ants, for the vast stretches of estate cane that fed the sugar factory in the south.

You see, cane was always there and we expected to live and burn our lives out in the field – less abruptly, perhaps, than my father who had passed away after being hit by a lorry carrying cane. My mother? Well, she gave up . . .

I was always home before Sis. Having brought the goats in, I did my homework sitting on the doorstep, hastening to finish it before the rest of the daylight faded. Then I climbed the boulder and watched for her.

Arriving, she would lower herself on the steps and I would hand her the big, white enamel cup brimming with water. My sister drank with a thirst – a gratefulness – I envied because she seemed to get such pleasure from a cup of water!

If working for the estate made water taste so good, that, for me, was reason enough to want to spend my life there also.

'You sister don wan you to work on no estate,' Tin Tin told me once.

Tin Tin was my friend – somebody I talked to and day-dreamed with freely. We were the same age and shared so much of our spare time together, I often forgot she was a girl who was therefore not supposed to throw stones, climb trees, pick fights and steal sugar canes. Yet, she could do all of these better than I. Worse, I couldn't beat her in a fight and was oftentimes obliged to retreat quickly into silence whenever our quarrels became too heated.

'My Sis didn say she don wan me to work on no estate,' I replied.

'She don have ter, chupidy! She sen yu to school, give you eddication; not so?'

'Your modder sen you to school too!'

'Yes, but she don expect me to – well, she not workin she soul-case out fo me. My modder different, see! Is you an you sister alone; my modder have eight o we. Sides, my fadder pass away.'

'My fadder pass away too!'

'Yes, but not in no sugar factory. Is a li'l ole truck dat bounce yours. Mines, is a whole factory!'

'Factory don bounce people,' I retorted, annoyed.

'I didn say dat,' Tin Tin was getting annoyed too.

'Nuh, but you implied that. If you assert . . . '

'Ass – sert,' she echoed scornfully. 'Big wud; you start showin off!'

'De wud jus slip,' I apologised.

'Slip what! You jus showin off coz you sister buy you big book an you done scholarship exams. You know damwelly if . . . '

She stopped short. But I knew what she was going to say. She was brighter than I. She used to be in the same class as I until The Accident. Would have been doing the exams too, had not her mother said that it made no sense. The two biggest boys would have to work in the field alongside her and she – Tin Tin – was not going back to school coz she couldn afford no school-expense and there wuz two little children to take care of durin' the day.

'Sis, how come Tin Tin cyah go back to school?'

'Ask er.'

'She tell me arready.'

'Don ask me, den.'

'She bright.'

'I know dat.'

'Nearly bright as me.'

Sis looked at me. This was one of the times when I felt she didn't like me at all.

'Nearly?' she asked.

My obvious discomfiture seemed to satisfy her. She ignored me for the rest of the evening.

The season deepened. What had once been growing canes became large expanses of parched straw as they were chopped down and the trucks and tractors took them away ton by ton.

Sis was one of the few who chopped cane. She did it because the choppers were paid fifty cents more than the loaders. It was very hard work but she had grown accustomed to it.

'Your sister is a chopper coz . . . ' Tin Tin seemed reluctant to continue

'Coz what?'

'Coz she in favour.'

'Ah don unnerstan.'

'Chupid boy! She have two overseer boyfren!'

'Don say dat bout my sister, Tin. I goin tell er!' I was hurt – deeply hurt. My sudden anger surprised me.

'Favour for favour, my modder say!'

'Don say dat bout my sister!' I was close to tears, in a fever; no longer afraid of her.

'Well, is what I hear say.'

Revenge, I thought. She was hurting me because she hadn't done the exams.

'She work same like everybody. Same-same-same!! *Harder* dan your modder an fadder put togedder!' I couldn't stop pounding my knee. 'Is not ongly man should chop cane fo money.'

'Okay, Baldie, awright. I didn't mean it. I sorry.'

'I goin tell er, you hear! I goin tell er.'

'Sorry, Baldie, sorry.'

'Don talk to me.'

We didn't speak for weeks. Tin Tin tried to make up to me several times and finally gave up, which disappointed me greatly since I had planned to soften a bit next time she came.

I tied out the goats, waited for Sis with her cup of water and studied her with a greater care – a deeper love, I think. I asked her no more questions; barely spoke. I was becoming like her.

I really missed Tin's companionship. More so, because the nights of the chill, bright moons had come. We should have been sitting with the rest of the village children on the mounds of cut canes, sucking away and talking about anything that came to mind.

We talked about the world, the things we had heard and read of – strange inventions, planes that flew backwards, machines that talked; wondering about all these and how our world of sugar canes fitted into it all; conscious of, but not questioning, the fact that our dreams for ourselves hardly ever went beyond the tallest canes.

Nothing compared with the pleasure we got from invading the fields of growing cane. You would hear the dull *Poks*! as we broke the soft stems, the swish of the swordlike leaves as we hauled the plant – root and all, into the road.

There was a watchman stalking somewhere in the night out there, but we didn't care. He never caught anyone. Besides, it didn't feel like stealing. There was something there though, as yet barely perceived, almost vengeful, in this act. We called it popping cane.

I had passed my exams; had done well enough to go to the secondary school of my choice. My name was even in the papers.

The following week, Tin Tin brought me a sapodilla. It was big, fat and ripe. It smelled so good, I almost fainted. It would be my first for the season. We often did this with our first fruit; we would come together and argue over the first bite. The first fruit was always the best. You got more than just its taste; you got the promise of a whole season of ripeness ahead.

I had suddenly forgotten our quarrel and all the weeks of not speaking to her. I wanted the first bite.

'I wan de firs bite.'

'Uh-uh,' she grinned.

'Gimme de firs bite, nuh.'

'You say, "nuh". Dat mean you don want it.'

'Yeh, man, gimme de sappo, nuh!'

'You say "nuh" again.'

'Jus one bite.'

'Okay, come for de bite.' There was a light in her eyes. I was blind to everything else but the fruit. I came forward. She opened her mouth and bit me hard. Tin Tin couldn't stop laughing. She then offered me the whole fruit. I ate half and offered her the rest. She shook her head.

I had never seen her so serious and easy-to-hurt before. I couldn't deny her a taste of our first sapodilla.

'Don want mo,' I said. 'I full up.'

'Tek it, I bring it for you.'

She was lying and knew I knew it. There must be a catch, I thought.

'What you want for it?' I asked

'Nuffing. Let's go an break cane.'

In a week or two, the season would be over. It was evening; I had already tied the goats in.

We had a favourite spot where we use to retreat to chew our cane and argue. It was the steps of what used to be a plantation house whose former immensity could still be judged by the colossal slabs of stones that made up its now decaying foundation and walls.

'You find ruins like dis all over de country, in all dem islands, always on de highest hill, lookin down,' I once commented to Sis, pointing at a similar picture in my history book. 'I wonder why nobody never bother to pull dem down or praps buil dem back?'

'Lots o things remain, besides dem old house,' muttered my

sister. 'If I have my way, I pull everyting down, dig up de foundation an start clean – start new!'

'Talk to me, Baldie,' Tin Tin said.

'Bout what?'

'Anyfing. Like we uses, erm; like we custom.'

'Bout when we get big, you mean?'

'Yup.'

'Okay, like I tell you; we goin buil a house wid – lemme see – nine room an . . . '

'No, ten – you say ten is a balance number, member?'

'Oh, yes – ten. And after?' I sought confirmation.

'Don ask me. *You* tell me.' She was suddenly angry . . .

'You ferget arready? You jus *start* goin to Secondary an you ferget arready! Go ahead.'

'An mebbe, mebbe we married, long as you don beat me up when I mek you vex,' I added.

'You never say "mebbe" before.'

'Well . . . '

'Wish I was a boy an didn have no lil brother an sister to care for. Then I woudda show you.'

'Is not my fault.'

'Is mines?' she snapped. She paused, then asked 'What you wan become?'

'Lawyer mebbe; praps doctor – make a lot o money.'

'You don wan to drive cane-truck no more?'

'Don fink so. Why you ask me all dem questions, Tin?'

'Cuz is not fair.'

'Is not my fault.'

'You say dat again, I rap you.'

'Well is . . . ' I stopped short. I thought I knew how she felt. I had never seen her so defeated before.

'I hate cane,' I said suddenly, viciously.

'Me too,' Tin Tin whimpered, close to tears. We rose and, together, picked our way over the stones of the same road that I watched the women travelling on every evening after work.

'Baldie,' she said shortly, her voice clear and strong again. 'I hate cane too. Cane not always sweet, you see. It have some dat salt, some dat coarse. It spoil you teeth; an if you not careful, you cut your mout wit de peelin. Take my fadder; take your fadder. See what happen? Dats why I don like no sugar in my tea. I fraid I might be drinkin im.'

She was talking like my sister. Did they all talk like that when things were not settled in their minds?

'I startin off on Monday, Tin.' I felt I had to tell her.

'I know.'

We were almost home. She smiled – her first for the day, I guessed.

'Luck, Baldie.' Tin Tin was looking into my face. She meant it.

'I see you tomorrow?' I begged, making a mental note to remember that it was ten rooms, not nine.

'Dunno, Baldie.'

'We goin break cane togedder, right?' I pleaded.

'Don fink so, Baldie,' she answered. She dropped my hand and sprinted off home.

If ever I needed Sis to talk to me, it was this time.

'Sis?'

'Huh?'

'Why Tin Tin tell me good luck as if I done dead o something? Like if she never goin see me again? She don even want to talk to me no more. She say if everybody can't get eddicated, den nobody should.'

'Coz she unnerstan.'

'Unnerstan what?' I demanded.

Sis looked at me then, and began to speak so slowly, you could barely see her lips move: 'Coz dem offerin you a chance – a ticket so's you could up an leave after; leave like you modder, *alone*, and never come back; leave everybody here, behind. Tin Tin shoudda gone before you – you know dat?'

I do not know how to say it, except that her eyes were burning. I mean it. Whenever she spoke like that, they seemed to gather all the lamplight and hold it in – sort of glowing. It

---

112

used to frighten me because she was no longer my sister when she became like this. She was somehow bigger and stronger and stranger than anyone I had ever known or dreamed of, staring past me, through the walls beyond the night. Beyond! . . . *I* didn't seem to matter as much as the thing she was staring at.

'What you want to become?' She had pushed the new uniform on the table in front of me as though I had only to put it on to become whatever I wanted.

'Tin Tin ask me de same question.'

'An you tell er?'

'Yep: doctor mebbe o lawyer.'

'No!!'

I looked up, surprised. Her eyes were still bright – still staring beyond me.

'We don need no lawyers now an we been gettin along fine widdout doctors. We wan teachers and a school firs!'

'But we talkin bout *me*; not no teacher an no school. Who it have to teach round . . . '

'We,' she hissed. I never knew a person's face could hold so many emotions at the same time. 'Teach, Baldie, coz Secandry ain't no real escape. Long as we tie down you tie down too. It ain't enough fo you to go alone. Learnin to escape cane not enough. How to *break* it – *break* out ov it, is what you have to learn. You unnerstan?'

I shook my head. I wasn't sure.

'Tin Tin unnerstan. *Sheez* de real canebreaker!'

'I could break cane too!' I was hating them for making me feel so confused.

'Den teach! Wen de time come, buil a school an stay right here an teach de children so'z it don have no mo Tin Tin; so'z it don have no mo *me* right? Canebreakers *before* lawyers!'

She was suddenly human again. The light had gone out of her eyes. I felt tired, washed out. I wished she hadn't thrown that weight on me, that she hadn't started me thinking and, for the first time, seeing the deepening lines of fatigue on her face.

I wished I would still experience the pleasure of handing her a cup of water and watching her drink away the day's hardship.

You see, she was pushing me to see things in a big, wide way, like Tin Tin sometimes did. As yet, I barely understood; but for once, my friends, I thought I glimpsed it – what she had been staring at that night, past me and beyond. And believe me, I was almost blinded by it. I looked at her and was shaken; even frightened by the power of such patience; the basis of such anger – so erm, no-no! I don have no regrets about anyfing: specially in this resolve I mek to remain.

Awright class there goes the bell. Straighten up now. Before you leave, please make a note of tomorrow's topic, It would help discussion if you read it at home in advance. Page forty-seven to fifty-two – Plantation Societies by P. Jameson.

What's that? Yes . . .

––––––––––

Jacob Ross was born in Grenada. He studied at the University of Grenoble, France. During 1979–83, he was Director of Cultural Affairs in Grenada. He now lives in London and is the Editor of *Artrage* magazine. He has contributed to several poetry collections and is author of a collection of short stories, *Song for Simone* (Karia Press, 1986).